I0619360

Early Exit

A Novel

Adam Patrick Donovan

Adam P. Donovan

This is for Camille. I miss you.

"Sometimes the only way out is through, and sometimes the only way through is love."
--ANONYMOUS

Contents

Early Exit

One

My neighbor always, always cooks bacon at six in the morning. I've only been here 90 days, but the dude hasn't missed a day. Today, I have him beat. My bacon is cooked and resting between two pieces of toasted sourdough and cheese, and it's barely five-thirty.

Technically, I'm not a consistent early riser; I simply didn't sleep. The night before, and the night before that—not a wink. There is something very, very wrong with my mind. Some of the old-timers told me this would happen. Out of the joint after 21 years at Pelican Bay, followed by 90 days in a halfway house, and now I've been on my own for 90 days—yes, six months out—and the snakes are already coming out of the basket.

The stinking thinking is on my ass.

Honestly, I feel like I'm riding out the tail end of a useless story that was basically over two chapters ago. I wrote past my natural ending.

I pack my sandwich in a brown bag and stick it in my backpack. No, I won't be eating the son of a bitch.

This is all just ceremony.

I also pack a small thermos of Sumatra coffee. I won't be drinking the coffee.

Yes, more ceremony.

In the tiny bedroom area of my apartment, I bring out my old man's World War II German Luger. I don't know where he got it. I only know he killed himself with it when I was thirteen. It's been mine for years. My lawyer friend, Morgan, held it for me while I was in the can. Being an ex-con on probation, I'm not supposed to have it. I have it now. I'm taking it with me today, and, believe me, this smoke wagon is loaded. Hell or high water, I'm going to use it, too.

I leave my apartment, lock the door, and go to my car. My car is a 2007 Toyota Corolla. A Little Old Lady from Pasadena kind of car. I bought it from a shy, older gal who rarely drove anywhere until she was too old to drive anymore. The little six-speed is 18 years old, with barely 11,000 miles on it.

Inside the car, I put the pack with the sandwich, thermos, and Luger on the seat beside me. I start the engine and go.

There's no self-talk salesmanship or self-soothing required for my task ahead. I'm all in, bought and sold. I know exactly what needs to be done and how I am going to do it.

Before Pelican Bay and the legal charges that sent me there, love had been good to me in the form of two entities—a woman and a child—who loved me and trusted me with two missions: to love them back and to believe in myself by loving myself a little bit more each day.

Simple enough.

I failed both missions.

The place I have picked for today is scorched earth: a section of Big Basin State Park burnt black from being ground zero of the largest firenado California has ever seen. A place that saw such temperatures, most of the old-growth redwood trees exploded.

There will be nobody there… I hope. The newspapers all say this area is off-limits—for years! Stay away. Give the green a chance to grow back.

The isolation there is what I seek. A space for dissolution and melting back into the earth, unbeknownst to anybody.

The drive takes me over an hour, and when I arrive at the charred trailhead, I see cars. Cars full of hippies, botanists, Audubon revelers—some with children.

Christ!

What are they doing? Didn't they read the warnings?

They are supposed to stay away and let the flora and fauna recover.

This will not do.

I leave.

The whole drive back to my apartment, I

self-soothe with a dark bedtime story I started playing for myself my first year in the joint. It's not a Mother Goose rhyme. More of a feeling. A dark flow. This feeling that I am the Minotaur of Crete, hidden deep in the belly of the labyrinth. What I did to Jeanie and Becky... I am a goddamn monster and belong there.

Being locked away in the labyrinth is tricky. Psychologically, it's a prison, and the only thing that breaks the monotony is when I get fed a sacrifice: a new sense of self. In between the sacrifices—although the labyrinth is dark and locked and fortified with the rock of self-loathing —tough guys and adventurers sneak in to kill me, to take my head. These starry-eyed adventurers are thought-forms, constructs of hope for light and love... someday.

But they don't catch me. They can hear me, see me in the periphery, feel my pain and longing, but all they get are the shadows.

Soon, these wannabe heroes and badasses tire and want out of the labyrinth.

Back at my apartment, I park the car, grab my pack, and go inside.

My apartment is funny. It's advertised as two bedrooms. One of the bedrooms is really a half-bedroom. I call it a mini-den. I sit on the futon in the mini-den and unpack the Luger from my pack.

I like it here in the mini-den, holding the Luger with its cold, heavy metal and the smell of sewing-machine oil in the barrel. This mini-den is now the center of the labyrinth, the belly. Nobody will see me or what's in here without looking. Yet you can't get out of the labyrinth by looking.

In the sense that "getting out of the labyrinth" is a euphemism for loving one's self, I have really been a monster. A magnanimous flop.

I change the Luger to my dominant hand, tighten my grip, and switch the safety off.

You must go within to get out of the labyrinth. To get out, you must go in and in.

I don't even feel the trigger be pulled—this close, it's that easy.

Two

"How long has it been?" she asks. Her eyes are blue fire, and she's sucking down her cigarette like she's starving. The darling can't wait to fire up the next ciggie. She makes the smoking look delicious. I want a cigarette, too, but I won't tell her this. "You look well—sturdy, calm, considering the circumstances. Maybe dangerous, too," she adds, exhaling as she speaks.

Dangerous?

What circumstances?

If she's trying to flatter me, this broad's communication style needs some work.

My memory needs work, too. Shit, I can't remember what I'm supposed to be talking to her about or why I'm here.

Who is this doll? She's gorgeous—spooky gorgeous. How did I get here?

We are at a truck stop in Barstow, California, where Route 66 and three other veins of forgotten America converge—a long way away from my apartment in goddamn Santa Cruz.

I know where we are the way I know my name is Frank Montu, the way the cherry blossoms know to burst with color in the depth of freezing winter. I also know we are at this crossroads of atrophied American dreams because, even though it's in the middle of the frickin' night, I can see outside the window, and there's a big, fat "Welcome to Barstow" sign.

"I think what you mean is how long have I been out of the can?" I tell her. I'm trying real hard not to stare at her cleavage. This isn't easy. Her skin is so white it is almost blue. Her blouse is buttoned low—way down, Mississippi-kind-of low —and the blouse widens as it rises all the way to the Arctic Circle.

Did I meet this gorgeous creature at some dive bar?

I have not done that in a while. I honestly don't remember.

A high-end courtesan is more my style.

Her hair is the color of wet raven feathers, flowing around the borders of her face and down her shoulders into an alluvial fade across her upper chest and shoulders. Although this woman could easily pass for having been carved from white marble, her face resembles that of Isabelle Boyer-Singer, the woman who modeled for the Statue of Liberty artists—especially her nose, chin, and brow.

I have not been with a woman in years, so I've learned to bury the urges, but this woman is already haunting me. The longings she stirs have festered in me year after year, and I have only known her for what feels like five minutes. It is her Old-World beauty that is breaking my heart open. Facial structure that belongs on cameo pins. The pale skin-to-dark-hair contrast on this creature is a perfectly complete marriage of innocence and darkness—she could be any madman's ink drawing.

"I've been out six months, if a day," I continue. "One day at a time, right? I am grateful for every minute of freedom."

I don't tell her this, but the first three months out of prison I was in a halfway house with a bunch of tweakers and junkies. I'm not an addict, and that was never my bag. I had to do a stint in some kind of state-funded transition place to appease the courts while I secured an apartment and started generating some income. I've only been free-free for about 90 days.

"I would like to hear what caused this," she says.

"Caused what?" I fire back. I know what she is after.

She wants to know why I was locked up in the first place. My guess is that Morgan told her some things, and who knows what exactly. He's helped me line up some work—driving jobs, thank God. For an ex-con, opportunities are skimpy. Morgan's been a lifesaver since my first day out.

"You know exactly what, tough guy. I

thought we were past all this."

I don't like how Ereshkigal is asking me to spill the beans, and the way she's asking me things is annoying as fuck. She's circling the drain, not coming at me directly. And I don't like how I know her name is Ereshkigal, and I can't for the life of me remember where I picked her up or how we got here. In Barstow of all places.

Maybe she picked me up.

"I am dense," I tell her. "Pretend I am dumb as a fucking rock, okay? Forget nuance. Everything you say, really spell it out for me."

"For my own comfort, Mr. Montu, I would like to hear you say it. Just a brief recap. So often third-party summaries are rife with inaccuracies. But more importantly, how you avow your past actions is important right now."

I don't say anything at first. I just stare. I can't read her, can't spot her tell, her angle for wanting me to barf up old news, my old life at Pelican Bay. She isn't after that gossipy relief of being pulled into someone else's dribble and melodrama. And she isn't jonesing for a crime-and-prison-story fix of tabloid-esque distraction. What I do detect is she needs a chore done, something only a desperado would agree to.

She needs a nasty favor from a nasty man like me.

She's not afraid of me. Not at all. There's something else. Something horrifying and relentless behind those blue-fire eyes.

How a fuckup like me might help is a goddamn mystery to me. I'm not the bodyguard type. I am 5'9", height-to-weight proportionate, Caucasian, neither handsome nor ugly. My eyes are brown—every kind of brown. You forget what I look like moments after meeting me. And I disappear into any crowd.

There is nothing remarkable about me.

I'd have to be an absolute moron not to see and believe this gorgeous creature is looking for a patsy of some kind.

Before I can even begin my *Reader's Digest* version of why I went to lockup, the doll picks up on more of my thoughts. "Mr. Montu, I ask because I have at times favored the personality who has, shall I say, rolled with the beasts and soared with the angels. I am trying to give you a chance to come clean."

"Look, love, I don't know about beasts and angels. I am flawed. Morgan's a good friend, and I am sure he did his best to stay close to the truth when he referred me. As far as coming clean, I don't know you, so how can I owe you anything? What's there to come clean about?"

Ereshkigal leans forward and stares into my eyes. I want to reach forward, gently grab the sides of her head, and lick her beautiful face. She is that lovely. Yet I know that in doing so, I would be embracing every nightmare I've ever experienced all at once.

The greasy spoon joint we are in feels cold.

I've never felt a place so cold. And it is only then that I realize there is no one else in this greasy spoon joint. Not a soul—just me and Ereshkigal.

I can't look at her eyes directly. If I look at her eyes directly, I will feel all the times I ever felt any kind of love come rushing to the surface.

It hurts.

I ruined all that love, again and again.

What I do to keep myself grounded in the booth seat: I look at that place just above her eyes. Basically, I stare at her eyelids and eyebrows. It helps a little.

Three

"**M**organ did not refer you, Frank Montu. I don't know why you keep thinking that. Nobody referenced you. You and I had a deal," she hisses at me. Her lips don't move, but she is telling me this, and her voice fills my head. "A deal before you came here. You broke that deal in a big way, and you know it! You broke our deal, Montu!"

"Deal? Woman, I don't even remember coming here, but I'm here. I don't know you, but I feel like I do, and you act like I do…" I want to tell her I feel like I've had some sort of psychotic break and that I'm not really here at all—I'm on some hospital gurney in some sort of coma or fugue state.

A waitress shows up at our table and delivers a ribeye steak so big the edges are hanging off the plate. She slides the plate in front of me. She also delivers a lowball glass of what is clearly two fingers of finer-quality bourbon—I can smell that glorious poison and can't wait to put it down.

"Did I order this?" I ask. I wave my hand

at the plate and bourbon. The waitress fades back into the shadows without a sound, and I keep my gaze aimed at Ereshkigal's eyebrows and wait for my answer.

"Tell me your side of things," Ereshkigal tells me. "I want to hear it. You don't remember our deal… fine. You will. Perhaps start with Jeanie."

Jeanie? Holy shit. How'd she pick that name out of the air? No name or utterance triggers more remorse and shame for me.

"Okay, babe," I answer. "Here's the deal: twenty years ago, right before I got sent away, I lived with the love of my life—Jeanie. How you picked that name out of midair, I could give a flying fuck. Jeanie had a six-year-old named Becky. Jeanie and I weren't married. It sure felt like we were headed in that direction. We had a small bungalow in Santa Cruz, the Seabright area, and every day was a dream. California dreaming."

I pause to shovel in a bite of steak. Good Lord. This steak is all the times I had the best steak coalesced into one steak. This steak is a dream.

I continue, "Becky started first grade at a school two blocks away from our bungalow. We were saving a few bucks each month. On weekends, we did outings. We even had a Disneyland run that first year together. We were three peas in a pod.

"Six months into the school year, Jeanie started allowing Becky to walk home from school with her pals. We had a sweet scenario. Norman

Rockwell would've painted our budding lives together. It was paradise…"

"Until it wasn't," Ereshkigal finishes for me.

I pause to try the bourbon. The bourbon is clearly bourbon from Heaven. Same as the steak: every sweet, wonderful bourbon memory I have is coalesced into the lowball glass I am holding and sipping from.

"One Saturday afternoon, a day warm and sweet as pie, Jeanie and I were cleaning the house and doing chores. Jeanie found a bag hidden in the back corner of Becky's closet. The bag had about sixty dollars in it—all quarters, half-dollar pieces, and silver dollars."

I pause after I say all that to give Ereshkigal time to intuit where I'm headed with this.

"That's a lot of money for that age," she tells me, nodding for me to continue.

"Gently, we asked Becky where it came from. Like all children, she cried and exaggerated and gave us odd stories. Wanting to be sure we were sure, after about sixty retellings, we finally had a version we knew was real."

"And you were able to find who gave her that money?"

"He was a demon," I answer back. "The only real kind of demon there is. Seifert Jennings. The man lived right around the corner. The moment I knew for sure he'd been giving Becky money, I knew what needed to be done. 'Pennies to Peek at Your Panties' was Seifert's game, and learning about it melted my brain.

"I grabbed a ball-peen hammer from the garage and went to see that Seifert Jennings was put by. I think you can fill in the blanks. I sent him out of the 3D, and then I went to prison. If a similar scenario unfolded, I would do it again."

Ereshkigal, the goddess of moonlit-ivory skin sitting across from me, doesn't pause a beat when I finish, and she tells me, "Your story doesn't surprise me a bit. You do have a code. I can also tell you are tired of being your story, yet you still wear it. What was once a uniform of moral code is now bulky and rusted armor, and you are unsure of its purpose and if you even want to wear it anymore. It's heavy."

I don't say anything. She's about to tell me I should keep my armor on, that I'll need it while performing some chore she needs completed. If she doesn't admit this with words, no matter; she's already saying it with her thoughts—that's how it feels just looking at her furrowed brow.

"Hmmm. You are leaving a lot out, Montu," Ereshkigal continues. Her voice sounds like it's coming from a defunct carnival ride from days gone by.

"If you are trying to flatter me, you suck at it," I tell her. "I'm a cliché, and I know damn well it'll take a while to outgrow the stigma. I'm smart as a fence post, full of remorse and self-deprecation, but I have had enough clarity to know I work best as a pacifist. I am not the chore boy or attack dog you are looking for."

"Thank you for the synopsis. I imagine you have run it in your mind millions of times by now, and I appreciate you playing the rerun for me."

Ereshkigal pauses here to light a new cigarette from the old cigarette. As she does this, she speaks with a bit of that marijuana voice people use—they speak without exhaling. "But you didn't tell me the whole story, the conclusion. You left that out. The conclusion's the best part, buddy. You've lived a life full of intense moments; why be a coward now? Tell me the last part, the denouement. It ties in nicely with our deal you can't seem to remember—our deal you breached!"

"What I think you are asking about is the worst part. You want to hear it? Fine, I'll tell you."

Ereshkigal doesn't answer, nod, or smile. She just fires those blue-fire bullets into my heart and soul and splinters my bones.

"I got to Pelican Bay, never heard a peep from Jeanie and Becky. Years later, I learned that Jeanie moved to Vegas. It wasn't until after I was out of the can and had some unadulterated access to the Internet that I learned what really happened to Jeanie and Becky."

I pause here.

My throat is so dry. Dusty kind of dry.

I reach for the bourbon, but it is gone. I cut off a piece of steak, but when I bring it to my mouth, I can see maggots writhing around. I don't say anything to Ereshkigal. She'll think my roof isn't nailed down very tight.

I set the bite of steak back on the plate.

"Just say it," Ereshkigal barks at me. "I want to hear you voice it with your heart and soul."

I try to cough, but I can't. I have never wanted water so badly in my life. Toilet water sounds delicious. I search the table, then I glance here and there nearby for the waif-like waitress.

"Say it with your voice," Ereshkigal repeats stiffly and loudly.

"The 'Jeanie and Becky moved to Vegas' rumors were crap. The reason I never heard from Jeanie: less than a month into my incarceration, before I was allowed visitors or communication with the civilian world, a woman with whom I had been having an affair and sneaking money to went by the cutesy bungalow there in Santa Cruz. She shared everything about our trysts with Jeanie. A few days later, Jeanie died in a car crash. Jeanie had been intoxicated and drove into oncoming traffic."

"And what of Becky?"

"I'm sure she died with her mother. Or not. I don't know. I couldn't read that far. If Becky survived—and what I did read did not make it sound like she's alive—that girl surely wants me to burn in hell. The devastation I've caused... I can only view it in small sips."

I stop there and look to Ereshkigal for mercy—water mercy.

"But that is not quite the ending, cowboy. There's one little piece. What did you do?"

"I didn't do anything."

"You and I had a deal where you would not come to see me. You were born into this world, and your mission was to stay and wait until I came for you. You broke it! What did you do? Say it loud and be clear!"

"I think it was today," I finally tell her with a voice that is barely a whisper. "Maybe it was yesterday. My timing is off. I put Pa's Luger into my mouth and smoked my own wagon. That's what I did. That's exactly what I did."

Ereshkigal smiles.

What horror.

She has too many teeth.

Four

"I completely get it. This is a decent start to the end of being dishonest with yourself," Ereshkigal coos to me. "We can actually start going somewhere if you can keep it up."

"I always drove us when we were together. Jeanie never drank. Drink and drive… not Jeanie's style. I got locked up, and there you go. If I had handled things differently, Jeanie and Becky would be alive."

"Stop whining," Ereshkigal tells me. "That stuff was twenty years ago. You keep trying to flatter yourself. Killing the child molester to defend Becky is one thing, absolutely. Jeanie and Becky learning that you had been milking through the fence the whole time you were telling Jeanie 'I love you' was the big poison."

The greasy spoon gets colder. Ereshkigal's voice is in my head, in the booth seat, in the table, coming down from the ceiling, and she still sounds like the voice of a defunct carnival attraction calling at me from way down at the end of a tunnel.

I try to defend myself against Ereshkigal's last jab, mention more about taking Seifert Jennings off the game board, but what comes out of my mouth in the faintest whisper is, "I was the big poison."

Ereshkigal continues, "You made the deal to wait for me to come to you and release you. You may not remember yet, but you are veiling it from yourself. Instead of keeping your promise, you tried to sneak out the exit."

"I killed a vile man, which in turn got the two beings I tried to protect and love the most an early exit." I know this is a distortion. Jeanie reacted the way she did when she learned I'd been giving money and sex to another woman.

"Shut up. Stop whining, Frank Montu. I won't tell you again. You have a choice. Since you came to me, and you didn't wait like we agreed, you can stay with me."

I thirst but can't drink.

I am hungry, but all the food is rotten.

I lust but can't embrace or love back.

I am cold, and there is only more cold.

This is what it is to be with Ereshkigal. I know I deserve it. I am like that king from the old stories: all that he laid his eyes upon turned to gold, but when he held anything close, it rotted.

Midas.

"The other avenue," Ereshkigal continues, "is you do me a favor. This'll save you from being

King Midas. The payment I will offer in return: you get to finish your ride and wait for me to come get you."

I try to answer her. My mind and its corrupt logic won't let me, and I keep getting knocked around mentally each time she pulls things right out of my head. This whole Barstow horror montage is simply not possible. I held Pa's Luger, and I did the dirty deed. I discharged that smoke wagon into my skull. How'd I get here? My brains surely scattered all over the mini-den wall in my cheapo Santa Cruz apartment. How is this Ice Queen here going to undo that mess?

"I bet you're curious about the favor part, the what's-in-it-for-you part?" she asks me.

I nod.

"Don't worry. It's an easy one. There's a youngster. Her name is Pigtails. She's just about what Becky's age would be now—a twenty-something. A royal brat, if you ask me. Her boyfriend, an absolute hosebag named Zipper, is about to rob a cash storage facility in San Jose. Not far from Santa Cruz. He'll eff it up and get shot while fleeing. His partner, a dangerous shitbird named Eightball, gets captured. Bleeding boyfriend hides the money and tells Pigtails, his girlfriend, where the money is.

"The boyfriend will then do two smart things before he bleeds out. He ditches the burner phone he uses to call Pigtails by torching it—turns it into ashes. Then the boyfriend does the same to himself and his van with white phosphorus."

Christ, this woman is macabre. What the fuck is her angle here? I had a cellmate for a few years. He'd been in and out of prison his whole life. He told me right before I was released, "About six months after you been out and doing good, a pair of big titties will come at you with a deal. Run, homie. Run for your life, unless you been missing lockup."

"Where are we going with this?" I garble out. "And when can I have some water?"

"You will let me finish, and you will make your choice."

I nod again. This demon is crackers. White phosphorus, armed stickups—none of this was ever part of my wheelhouse.

Ereshkigal continues, "Pigtails goes and grabs the haul boyfriend tells her about before he dispatches himself. She checks all the bank straps for GPS trackers and runs back to her apartment. Her plan is to go somewhere like Vegas, LA, New York. Somewhere with crowds and crowds. The idea is to launder the money while buried in a maelstrom of sheep.

"She'll be back at her apartment, scared, reactive, and packing up in about two hours. Your task, Montu, is to stop her from going to Vegas. And if you can't stop her, go with her and sway her away from the lower roads."

"This is odd. Why do you say that? She wants a life of crime; that's her choice. You seem like a freedom-of-choice proponent."

"I really have no feeling about it. Pigtails' boyfriend's partner, the one who gets captured in the botched robbery, gets out on bail thanks to rich daddy, and he goes after Pigtails. My preference is to pick her up at a later age—a much later age—as opposed to next week. If Eightball gets her, I'll be seeing her next week."

"Look, babe. I can't control Pigtails. I don't know her and don't want to know her. I can't protect that girl, I can't control her away from certain lifestyles—shit, I put my own self by a few hours ago."

"You are correct," Ereshkigal adds. "You have zero ability to control her. You are a flop at protecting others."

The pain of Jeanie killing herself, and possibly Becky, while driving drunk because I tried to protect them by killing Seifert Jennings floods to the surface. Man, I was a cheater that whole time.

"But you can inspire Pigtails, Frank Montu. Zero control, but unlimited ability to inspire. Did I mention Pigtails is exactly the same age Becky would be if that chain of events you set off never happened?"

"I think you enjoy prodding my pain spots," I tell her. "You keep pushing the wounds to get me to say yes and flinch in some way."

"I am being generous, Francis Daniel Montu. I am giving you a chance for some redemption while doing me a favor. You don't have to. You can keep this early exit and stay by my side —thirsty, hungry, longing for love, ad nauseam. I think you might grow to enjoy the crossroads, the between place we are right now."

"I'll do it," I tell her. "I'll do it. I'll give it a shot. I can't possibly do worse than the track record I have. Anything is better than this moment."

"You're right about that," she sasses back.

"You suck at boosting someone's self-esteem. You really do. What is the fine print of this deal?"

"There's no fine print. Do your best to sway Pigtails, inspire her toward a higher road. Stay with your body until I come get you. No early exits!"

I am about to ask her about a tricky topic. That Luger would have done a number on my skull. How's she going to work around that? Am I going to have to wear a hat everywhere?

"One last thing," she adds. "The body you will use and stay with until the day I come to get you is not the body you had. The body you had isn't serviceable."

"You better explain what you just said," I tell her. "You're outside of my zip code of comprehension right now. I told you, you need to explain things like I'm dumb as a rock."

"Rocks, minerals in general, are very intelligent, but this is a topic for a different time, perhaps. You can't use the body you were using. You ruined it. Therefore, in about twenty minutes exactly, in downtown Capitola, California, a man named Bobby 'Dynamite' Dixon is going to OD on heroin. He will then stay with me, and you will use his body."

"Dynamite Dixon? What the fuck is that? This dude a celebrity or something?"

"Almost, almost famous. More of a punching bag. If he managed his time better, stayed away from opiates, he could have been a contender or a lower-rung gatekeeper type."

"Is he one of these MMA cats you see on TV?"

"No. Boxing. Washed-up boxer. His body will be a little banged up. You'll be just fine inspiring Pigtails. Bobby Dynamite will flatline out behind a water heater at a sober-living house. That's where you come in—"

"What, I just wake up behind a water heater, just like that? No more blown-out skull. I'm a boxer who's... had his day and likes to stay sleepy? You are giving me some funky cards to try and win with."

Ereshkigal has no energy or answer for my sarcasm. How she answers is through my body. First my feet go numb, then my legs, my waist. I feel like I am melting into the booth seat and the floor.

"I get it," I tell her. "I'll cut the crap. You're gorgeous. Mesmerizingly gorgeous, and scary as hell. But you do realize everything you just told me sounds cray-cray, right?"

"Here's an Ace, if you need it, if your lovely charm is not enough. Pigtails loved her Grandma Katie. Grandma Katie was always whispering old stories about growing up in Scotland. Use that, Montu. Get creative with it."

Five

Eyes of blue fire wasn't joking when she said I would wake up in a body passed out behind a water heater. I am on my side, staring right at a dirty Maytag label peeling with rust and age. I can see the flicker of the pilot light's reflection bouncing off the concrete floor beneath me and the water heater. I can hear the tick and hiss of water boiling.

It takes some effort—moving-through-thick-mud kind of effort—to sit myself up. My left arm is tied off with an old belt, and there's a needle with the plunger pushed home sticking out of my arm. I grab that thing and give it a good fling. I wince at the noise it makes as it clatters against the wall and floor of a nearby corner, remembering that I am in some sober-living place, and I need to get out of here with zero delay and zero attention from others.

Standing is not easy. I use the wall. My legs feel like oatmeal. All my muscles feel like cold, clumpy oatmeal. After a few seconds to acclimate to standing up, I gently slide myself toward the door, using the wall as a brace.

The room I am in has two mop buckets, a deep sink, and a wobbly-looking floor-to-ceiling shelf with all sorts of cleaning crap—sponges, squirt bottles, etc. There's a mirror above the sink.

Hell no! I will not look at that mirror.

Not until I feel strong. Bobby "Dynamite" Dixon—no offense, brother—but I am going to melt down when I see myself as you. So, no mirrors until I have some chutzpah back. I want to see what kind of body I am wearing, but I don't. It feels like my body, but there are attributes that are alien.

Above the mirror is a bumper sticker that reads, "Easy Does It." One of the more popular AA slogans. Lucky for me, I recently finished a short stint at a halfway house as part of my requirement for release from Pelican Bay. I have never been here before, but I have a vague idea of what the lay of the land might be: two occupants per room, a house manager, a clipboard in a central location listing chores and dates for chores to be completed —possibly cleaning teams with names of members and room assignments.

I check my pockets. No wallet. No keys.

First on my agenda is finding Bobby Dynamite's room and hopefully finding his wallet, which is technically my wallet. Maybe he's got a cellphone.

Second on my agenda is to get to the bar in downtown Santa Cruz called The Tiki Room.

Pigtails lives in a small apartment above The Tiki Room.

Third on my agenda—and certainly the most important—is to find a clock. Ereshkigal said I'd have just under two hours to get out from behind the water heater and get to The Tiki Room to intercept Pigtails. How much of my narrow window of time have I burned up here doing the dope-fiend lean against the wall?

I have no idea.

I scoot myself down the wall until I am up against the door. I press my ear against the door and listen.

I don't hear any sound.

What I hear is ambiance. Daytime ambiance. The quiet hum of work hours—the range between 9 a.m. and 5 p.m.

Here goes nothing.

I turn the knob and open the door.

This place smells like a halfway house.

What does a halfway house smell like? Cheap cologne. Bleach. Cigarettes. Coffee, like a pot just brewed. And the faint hint of essential oils. This halfway house is likely a coed version.

Straight in front of me is a door. All around the doorframe, you can see how the locks have been changed a thousand times or so. To my left is a staircase. There's a light on at the top of the staircase. I am in no condition to go up that staircase.

To my right is an open door to a dining area.

I can hear noise coming from the dining area—someone in there rustling with things.

My Spidey senses tell me there's a kitchen attached to the dining area. One or two parties are in the kitchen area preparing or cleaning.

I know I walk like Frankenstein, but this is the best I can do. Slow at first, then I pick up some momentum, some speed to my gait. I shuffle toward the dining area.

Through the doorway and into the dining area, I can see the creator of the noise: a tall, lanky Black man. The gentleman is fussing with a blender. He's got a tub of something next to a pile of celery and some other leafy stuff. You'd think the man was shooting a porno for rabbits and tortoises. This is all being done on a long Formica bar that separates the dining area from the kitchen area.

I step into the dining area far enough that I am in the blender man's periphery. He looks up.

"Dynamite, look at you. I ain't seen you all day."

"You see me now," I tell him.

I don't mean to sass him like that. Having a body in slug-mode because of too much dope has me agitated. My voice sounds alien—it has a street-talk bounce to it. So far, I am not liking this experience of being Bobby Dynamite.

"I may need your help with something," I tell the blender man.

Six

Finally, I can see a digital clock on the wall. It says 2:30 p.m. Funny. What feels like just twenty minutes ago, I was talking to Ereshkigal at a greasy spoon place in Barstow, and it was the middle of the goddamn night.

"Of course, boss," the blender man answers. I watch him finish dumping his large scoop of green stuff into the blender pitcher. "What do you need?"

"I need you to run to my room and grab my wallet."

"Your wallet?"

"Yes. My wallet and my cellphone."

The blender man shakes his head. "Man, I didn't know you had a phone."

"Fuck the phone. Just grab my wallet for me. That's all."

"Is there something going on, dude?" the blender man fires back. His brow is furrowed as he scans me up and down.

"Nah, man. I pulled something in my back.

I'm not sure I can do the stairs just yet. I'm going to try to see somebody, maybe."

"And you're sure your wallet's in your room?"

"Yes."

"Hey, I'm about to hit some of this smoothie —I jacked it full with super greens. Got this all loaded with algae, too. You want a glass?"

"Algae? Like pond-scum algae?"

"Yeah, man. Celery juice, spirulina, kale, and some lemon. You want a glass?"

"Not if my throat were on fire. I really need my wallet, bro."

"I can't do it, boss," the blender man answers, shaking his head again. "You know the rules. Unless you're in your room, I can't enter."

"I'm *asking* you to go into my room."

"Can't do it, homie. Rules are rules. I'm almost out of here. Don't want any trouble at this stage in the game."

"Fuck the rules."

"See, now you sound like you need a meeting or to call your sponsor. You sound like the snakes are coming out of the basket. You got the stinking thinking wagging your chin."

"A goddamn boa constrictor's coming out of the basket. I'm in pain here. If you get me my wallet, I can go to urgent care. Please."

"Your roomie ain't up there?"

"Fuck that guy."

The blender man closes his eyes, rests his

chin on his chest. After a long pause, he says, "Wait right here, captain. If it ain't out where I can see it, you're shit out of luck. And one other thing—you got the 'fuck-its' right now, real bad. None of my business, but you should call your sponsor. There's not a fool alive who doesn't know that the 'fuck-its' are a relapse symptom."

"Deal. I love you for this. You are right. Get me my wallet, and I'll go straight to my sponsor and then urgent care."

I look up at the clock again. I have an hour and a half to get to Santa Cruz, find The Tiki Room bar, and situate myself near whichever entrance leads to the upstairs rental. This is the simple task. The complicated task is to convince a twenty-something to trust me to help her launder the stolen swag her boyfriend died attempting to lift in a strong-arm robbery—and to steer her away from a "lower road" and a homicidal psycho named Eightball.

Seven

The vantage point I've hidden myself in is a low stack of pallets beside two dumpsters. From here, I can see The Tiki Room's rear entrance and a set of exterior stairs leading up to the second floor. There's a banged-up, scuffed blue door on the second floor with a narrow balcony connecting it to the stairs. Next to the blue door is a faded sign with the number and letter: 1B. There's also a low bench next to the door with a few pairs of shoes on it. Whoever lives there, well, they want you to take your shoes off before you come in.

I walk around the building twice, even sneaking a couple of bumps of bourbon from the bar. If there's a 1A, I can't find it. I am pretty damn sure 1B is where Pigtails hangs her pigtails each night, so I waddle back to my nook between the pallets and dumpsters.

I have no idea how deeply Bobby Dynamite had fallen off the wagon before he overdosed, but since I'm using his body now, my big concern is getting dope sick while I'm trying to sway Pigtails.

Bobby's wallet contains a driver's license and two boxing licenses: one from the California State Athletic Commission and one from the Nevada State Athletic Commission, both from nine years ago—a bit of a sentimental fella. There's also a VA medical card and $175. I took a twenty and bought myself a pint bottle of whiskey and some cigarettes—to take the edge off being dope sick, if that starts to happen.

My only consolation is knowing from personal experience that you can't get too janky without getting booted from a halfway house. Bobby still had a room at that halfway house he shared with the blender man and others—hence, the withdrawals coming for me might not be too bad; he likely wasn't too deep into relapse land.

A boy can hope.

Off to my right, I watch a car with an Uber placard on the dash pull over about a half-block away. It makes me think the passenger is getting out to visit the Chinese restaurant right there, Ming's.

The passenger who exits the Uber is wearing mini-mini shorts and combat boots, a sports bra with a lace bra over the top of it, and —you guessed it—her hair is done in bright blue pigtails. There must be at least fifty necklaces hanging from her neck, and just as many bracelets on each wrist. She's as muscled up as a car antenna.

I watch her shoulder a green Army-style duffel bag with arms like coat hangers, covered in tattoos.

The bag looks heavy as hell—weighted-down-with-swag kind of heavy.

Good Lord. I'm in trouble.

I take a quick nip from my pint bottle, a deep drag from my cigarette, and ready myself. Big moments are not my favorite, but this is my big moment about to arrive.

Everything is riding on this next conversation about to happen. If I butcher it, she'll flee to Vegas or somewhere crazy, and I'll be Ereshkigal's dinner guest—forever!

Watching who I believe is Pigtails walk toward me saps all my confidence. Each step is not gangly like you'd expect from a woman who's a bit tall, young, and has both body and limbs shaped like wood dowels. This youngster lands each step with the precise gusto you would need if you were trying to shove your foot through the sidewalk.

As soon as she's within earshot, I flick the cigarette away and try my pitch.

"Pigtails, I need to talk to you in private. You pick where, just somewhere we aren't out in the open like this."

She pauses and stares at me for what seems to be the longest time. Something in her face is familiar—so familiar. Something from long ago—the Jeanie days.

"I don't know you. I don't know you," she fires back.

"No. You don't. You are spot-on correct

about that. I am sorry about your boo. His buddy, however, won't be in lockup long. Eightball, right? A nasty bastard. He'll be out, you bet…"

"Look, Punchy, pack sand or I'll scream. I do not know you or these names you are barfing out."

Pigtails starts edging and sidestepping closer and closer to the bar entrance. She's bolting any second now. I need to get this right or all is lost.

"Grandma Katie—that girl always wanted you to go to Scotland. Flights go every day. I will help you launder things, and you will be in Glasgow before the weekend. Get you an expedited passport, too—I know how to do that."

Eight

"Ereshkigal? Never heard of her," Pigtails snaps back. "Sounds like a real biatch. Spell it for me, please."

"E-R-E-S-H-K-I-G-A-L."

"Never heard of her. And I was right—total Fucking Karen name. I don't know how you know what you know, but a few things are bang-on. I promised Nana years ago that I would see Scotland, come hell or high water. I know something went down with Zipper and Eightball. Zipper left something for me in our hidey-spot, and I grabbed it when he called me and told me to go there. You say Eightball's in lockup, and I believe you. Greasy as hell, I know he is. He'll be out.

"As for Zipper being dead... I'm not saying a peep until I'm sure. I like to believe he has nine lives. No crying until I know, and I'm not going to look for any indication of Zipper's status until I have what he left me laundered and secured—a girl can do a lot from somewhere like Glasgow.

"This laundry stuff... I know what I know.

What do you know, Punchy?"

"I know a thing or two."

"Yes, but your thing is not my thing."

"I got three methods that launder quickly and will keep the attention off you," I answer her.

A total lie, too. I know nothing about money laundering. A lot of dudes in the can talked about all their scams and schemes, but I never listened. Hey, shit—if they were that good, they wouldn't be jawing into my ear while in the hoosegow, trading tats for tuna packets and Ramen.

We are in 1B above The Tiki Room bar, sitting at the tiny kitchenette table. On the table between us, there's a toaster with a dangerously frayed cord, a fishbowl with water that is bright green. Every once in a while, a bulging-eyed fish swims close enough to the glass that I can see him.

Three or four ashtrays are parked here and there within arm's reach of the table, empty beer bottles everywhere, clothes on the couch, and two skateboards leaning against a wall. Yes, Zipper must be a real dreamboat to have around.

Despite the place being an absolute pigsty, Pigtails made me take my shoes off and leave them outside on a bench by the door.

"Look here, Punchy, you're pitching for me to take you with me so you can get some imaginary biatch off your back if you somehow protect me from Eightball. Frankly, you look like my dad or my grandpa's age—and dope sick. Eightball will put you into the ground. You better sell me on your knowledge about laundering, and it better be good. I'm already in the camp of leaving you behind, and I'm leaving in ten minutes. Time's not on your side."

She stands from the table while dishing out her warning to me. I watch her grab a backpack, dump the contents onto the couch, and start rifling through the drawers of a bureau next to the bathroom door.

Sonofabitch, Ereshkigal was spot-on correct.

This skinny, tall thing has so many nuances that Becky had, it's hard not to trance out on her while she packs. The way she smiles and moves, holds her shoulders, shrugging while she talks. She's Becky, and she isn't Becky—this really feels weird, and it hurts. I feel like I am being reunited with a daughter I thought was lost, but I never deserved to have her in my life in the first place.

I don't answer fast enough, so she jumps in and barks at me over a bony shoulder, "You have ten seconds to tell me your laundering gambits, or you gotta go, Punchy."

"Three methods I know that work," I tell her. "First method: go to a casino, grab nine grand in chips, walk around a couple of hours, then turn the chips back in and cash out. Staying just below ten grand keeps you under the tax-reporting limit."

"That's lame and overused. I'll use it, but

come on, man—you're making me yawn here. Besides, you don't even have to use the cages anymore—use ATM-like machines and bar-coded tickets. I think you've had your day, homie."

"In addition to the first method, we purchase pre-charged credit cards. You bring cash on the flight to Scotland—customs over there will zoom in on why you are showing up with a suitcase full of cash. Pre-charged cards scan through the X-ray machines looking exactly like what they are: pieces of plastic, gift cards from all your boyfriends. Have some in your wallet, some in the suitcase, some in your bag. FedEx a boxload to the hotel you'll be staying at in Glasgow, attention: care of guest, blah, blah, blah."

"Okay. Another gambit straight out of a Cracker Jack box. You are zero for two, buddy. One more strike and you're out."

"The third method goes like this: we use sportsbook betting. Pick a sportsbook; it doesn't really matter which one. Say the 49ers are playing. I take nine grand and bet that they win. You bet nine grand that they lose. Your winnings will be eighteen grand or more, and you pay five percent to the house. Do it like that. Do it at many sportsbooks, and launder everything in a day—we got football season cracking right now."

"Now that is still a rookie method, but not bad. Not enough, however, to bring your washed-up ass with me. Too much risk."

I watch the way she moves, the shape of her

jaw—so many subtleties—when she says all this. I am pretty sure I am losing cabin pressure because I see nothing but Jeanie and Becky in this girl.

Shit. I need something. Some leverage to inspire her to bring me along.

What I have, which is ironic, is the one thing Jeanie and Becky needed from me... but I was locked up in Pelican Bay and couldn't give it to them when they needed it most.

A ride.

Frank Montu, who I was just twenty-four hours ago before I killed myself, has an apartment and car here in Santa Cruz.

How do you like that?

"The best reason to bring me along," I tell Pigtails. I do my best to say it smooth, not desperate. "You need a ride. You need a ride because laundering that swag and driving to Vegas is going to be many stops. And you need a ride that isn't connected to Zipper, Eightball, or you. And you need a reliable ride because the last thing you want is to sit on the side of the desert freeway with 2.5 million in freshly heisted scratch. Who knows what a nosy chippie or tow truck driver might pull."

"And you have the perfect ride?" she sasses back.

"No. I don't."

"Then what are you getting at, knucklehead?"

"Frank Montu has a fine ride."

Hearing myself say these things out loud is a real mind-bender. I'm talking from Bobby Dynamite's body about using the car owned by the me that I was just a day ago before I killed myself.

"Fuck Frank Monkey, or whatever his name is. He can go hump his own leg. Meeting you was enough. I'm not mixing in any more… outpatient program people."

"His car's in a driveway about two miles from here. I can use it all I want—take it to Vegas, wherever. I'll drive, you sit in the seat behind me. I get out of line the slightest bit, you slam me, blast me, stab me. You'll have all the control."

She doesn't say anything.

"Hey, girl, we switch that cash over, you fly straight to London, and then Glasgow. I will show you how to file for an emergency passport."

"I have a passport, if I can find it. The gov websites have all the answers on that stuff anyway, Grandpa."

"You need me," I tell her.

I know I'm shooting from the hip. I also feel like I am getting the flu or a cold or both—dope sickness. My hope is that it doesn't worsen, and if it does, she doesn't see.

"I'm your patsy," I continue. "You get pulled over, nailed with all that cash, tell 'em I took you against your will. I'm your fall guy."

"Keep going," she interjects. "This is a first. The first thing out of your mouth that makes sense. This and the car idea, although I don't want that Frank Monkey guy involved."

"Montu. Frank Montu. He's away. I'm watching his things. You'll never meet, see, or even hear Frank Montu's voice. I'll be your driver and your fall guy. Crazy-ass Eightball shows up, I run the interference. You're right—I'm old and washed up. I can, however, interfere and slow him up. Same with Ereshkigal. You don't know her. But she knows you—who do you think told me that stuff about Nana Katie? Eightball, law enforcement, whoever comes after you, I'm your interference."

"You must think I'm some kind of monster?" she asks.

Both the freshly packed backpack and the Army seabag loaded heavy with cash are sitting by the door. She lights a new cigarette and gives me a deep stare, waiting for my answer.

"Why do you say that?" I ask. "I'm telling you how I can help."

"I asked you to sell me on your value, and you are appealing to my interests by explaining how I can feed you to the wolves and buy myself some time. Like you're okay with falling on your sword, taking an early exit."

Early exit?

Didn't Ereshkigal say something like that?

"That's right. I've had some success with that, you might say."

What I don't tell Pigtails is the real answer. The sad answer. The truth is, I had and still have a lot of love to give. I messed up my opportunity to give it to the two people I wanted to give it to.

Maybe spending some of that love while helping Pigtails will put me in a better dimension within myself before Ereshkigal comes to collect me.

Nine

Our first step is to Uber to a small park two blocks from the apartment I occupied when I was the late Frank Montu—the version of me from just twenty-four hours ago. We decide it is best to avoid any direct connections to Montu's apartment—even an Uber driver knowing could be a link—hence the drop-off two blocks away. And since Frank Montu has only been dead for about a day, I know I will be relatively safe entering the apartment to grab the car keys, cash, and whatever else might be useful—after all, it is technically mine, even if I am no longer in Frank Montu's body.

The Frank Montu body is surely still in the mini-den, and I will do all I can to avoid looking at it.

The walk from the park to my former apartment is quick but unnervingly tense. It feels like everything is watching us—the flowers, the trees, the birds. Even the sun and breeze seem to be monitoring every step. I feel like the universe is suspended in a between-place, caught between inhalation and exhalation.

I can tell Pigtails senses it too. Even though she walks behind me, I notice her wary glances from side to side, smoking incessantly.

I don't have my old keys or any personal items from my time as Frank Montu, but I vividly remember where the spare key is hidden.

How could I forget?

I also remember the final act I had taken as Frank Montu, and Pa's Luger, which is why I insist Pigtails wait outside while I go in to retrieve the car keys. She doesn't need to see what is inside that mini-den.

Inside the apartment, I make sure to breathe through my mouth to avoid the smell of death, and I steer clear of the mini-den with the futon. I quickly grab the Toyota Corolla keys from a basket in the kitchen and Montu's stash of cash from a cookie jar next to the toaster oven, and then I am out of there.

Sitting in the late Frank Montu's 2007 Toyota Corolla is unexpectedly emotional. Nostalgia, warmth, and longing wash over me. I had bought this reliable, unassuming car right after my release from prison from a Little Old Lady from Pasadena who had barely put eleven thousand miles on it. At the time, I felt really lucky finding this car—like there was luck and hope for me.

Pigtails, beside me and looking and feeling like Becky, stirs renewed hints of luck and hope that whisper at me.

I start the car and pull out of the apartment complex parking lot. I am silent as the moon, even though it is late afternoon, and Pigtails lets me have this.

Frank Montu is dead, and his body will be found soon. The me that is Bobby Dynamite knows I won't be back. Intuitively, I know that the car and I—this little car that once represented hope and a new beginning—will find ourselves facing a nasty and violent ending while distracting the array of characters who will be coming for Pigtails' stash.

Pigtails will get away. I know that, and I won't let her see my next exit.

And when I lie there in the dust and blood, staring up at the desert sky, I will dream that I had a daughter, that I loved her, and that she is happy somewhere far away and safe—like Glasgow —because, for once in my goddamn life, I actually had a moment where I did the right thing.

Ten

Our next destination is an adult bookstore in downtown Seaside, California, about forty miles from Santa Cruz. This is Pigtails' idea—not mine—and I wish it had been my idea because it is brilliant. The bookstore has a section filled with BDSM gear: handcuffs, whips, and other paraphernalia. Not my scene—I have never been into any kind of porn, so none of this resonates with me.

Pigtails purchases two hefty sets of handcuffs. I stand there beside her with my flat, crooked nose, dope-sick, sweating self, trying to figure out how in the world I am going to protect Pigtails when the baddies show up, and I know they will be coming.

Back in the car, as we head toward Vegas, she sits directly behind me, one set of cuffs securing her ankles. She plans to use the second set on her wrists, covering herself with a blanket at the first sign of being pulled over. This setup will support the story I promised her earlier: if questioned, I will take the fall, make her appear as a hostage rather than an accomplice to Zipper's strong-arm robbery cash haul.

Our third stop, which includes refueling, is a large Love's truck stop just outside Bakersfield on Highway 99.

The plan is to remove the cuffs from her ankles for a stretch, and I will covertly check for any news on Eightball—is he in custody or still at large? Using the late Zipper's Samsung tablet —which, ironically, has more bookmarks for porn sites than I thought possible—I search for updates on Eightball, Zipper, and their botched robbery.

The heist had been executed only eight hours earlier, and details are scarce. A brief mention of a "person of interest" being questioned is all I find—nothing concrete about Eightball or any suspects being apprehended.

Pigtails and I grab some cheeseburgers and Diet Cokes. She wants to smoke a few more cigarettes before we continue, since I won't let her smoke in the car. I join her in her cigarette binge, trying to calm my jittery, achy body with nicotine.

My attempts to eat are hampered by cloying waves of dope-sickness nausea. To distract myself, I try again to gather information about Eightball. Pigtails does her best to fill me in with what she knows.

Eightball is a thirty-year-old California native from a wealthy wine family, with a criminal past that includes suffocating a cousin and a subsequent charge of maiming. Here in California, a maiming charge is reserved for assaults that disfigure another person or persons.

This history doesn't bode well for me—a worn-out body no match for Eightball's brutality. On the hopeful side, I do have my time in the can and what I learned there: how to punch, kick, bite, and eye-gouge to survive.

As we prepare to leave the truck stop, I watch Pigtails through the car-window reflection, smoking and staring at the sky, her figure overlapping with memories of Becky and Jeanie. I don't know how I will protect her. I hope to buy enough time to launder the stolen cash and get her on a flight to Glasgow before either Eightball catches up or law enforcement starts connecting the dots to Zipper's associates.

Reflecting on my own reflection, I see a man far removed from his past life: a halfway-house cretin who's had his day. Five-foot-nine, visibly aged, with a battered nose and jailhouse tattoos marking a life of hardships.

I think about Bobby Dynamite's likely experiences—never far from a drunk tank or detox —and feel the irony of my situation: inhabiting the body of a man who, like me, had ended his own misery, giving me a chance to perhaps right some wrongs.

As we drive away from Love's, leaving behind the truck stop for the vast stretch of highway to Vegas, I feel a mix of fear and anticipation. This journey with Pigtails is not just about evading the law or outmaneuvering a criminal like Eightball; this is a morsel of redemption, about offering the kind of support and love I had failed to give Jeanie and Becky.

Despite the uncertainty, my physical discomfort, and a body that's had its day, there is a glimmer of hope—that perhaps, in these final acts, I can find a semblance of peace or, at least, a sense of purpose in the borrowed time I have left.

Eleven

"You having second thoughts now?" Pigtails asks.

"What makes you say that, homie?" I respond, watching her through the rearview mirror. Her face remains glued to the burner phone we picked up at the Love's truck stop—a brief pause in our journey. Frankly, I can't wait for the next pause. No burgers and ciggies for me; I'm taking a goddamn nap, and the royal highness will have to wake my ass up when she's ready to roll.

"I'm not your homie, so don't say that," Pigtails sasses back. "I ask because you've been lost in space since we left Love's. You're like a stroke victim or something—one of those boomers who eat weed gummies to manage their emotions."

I'm too tired to concoct a story. It's simpler to just share the truth gnawing at my mind. "The main idea is you remind me of the daughter of a woman I loved and would have married. I messed it up. Helping you now gives me a sense of redemption. I mentioned some of this earlier."

"Shit, you're getting distant now because you've seen just what kind of crazy Eightball is. He's coming, and you know it."

True to form, she doesn't look up from the burner when she says this, but I can feel her dying for me to respond or defend in some way.

"I'm sure he's quite a specimen. I'll capture his attention, divert it, and you'll make it to Glasgow," I assure her, though she remains focused on her phone, scared and trying not to show it.

I am scared, too.

She's looking for more reassurance, and I don't know how to give it to her. The likely outcomes are stark:

· Eightball catches us, and I fail Pigtails.

· The authorities find us—though they're not yet looking for Pigtails—and our ruse

collapses, landing us both in custody.

· Or, the outcome I'm aiming for: I help Pigtails launder the stolen money, she starts anew in Glasgow, and I lead Eightball and any pursuers on a wild goose chase.

But how exactly do I start and lead this chase?

I haven't a clue. As soon as someone nasty makes their move, I bet I'll have plenty of ideas.

"I like our plan," I finally tell her, trying to bolster her spirits. "We'll load you up with plenty of prepaid credit cards. Put some in your backpack, a couple in your wallet. We'll purchase them sporadically, always staying under nine grand. We'll do the same with Western Union. Tomorrow, Bobby Dynamite will wire you nine grand to a Glasgow station, and you pick it up in local currency when you get there. Easy. Then, from another Western Union, you send yourself another nine grand. Rinse and repeat. We'll also hit some sportsbooks; after, you deposit the winnings into various online cash apps, keeping transactions under nine grand. Plus, we'll grab nine grand in traveler's checks from Triple-A." I add with a laugh, "Christ, no haggis for you. Your first few days in Scotland will be spent visiting numerous banking centers and Western Unions, converting traveler's checks."

"I can't tell if you're trying to soothe me or overwhelm me."

"I need you to win probably more than you need to win."

"That's right. I almost forgot. You are making amends to all the 'could have been' moments with Becky and Jeanie you wrecked."

I don't answer. She's right.

"Sorry, bro. That was mean."

"No apology necessary," I tell her. "You are spot-on. I am exploiting the help that you need in hopes of eroding the guilt I feel that weighs about a ton. Frankly, it's crushing me."

"You haven't mentioned Ereshkigal since this afternoon."

"I only want to focus on things we can control," I say, steering the conversation away from uneasy topics.

Pigtails asks, "You said she was going to come for you. Ereshkigal, that is. What do you mean by that?"

It strikes me as odd that Pigtails asks this just as we pass through Barstow—a place that chills me to the bone. This synchronicity makes me feel as if Ereshkigal is near: in the car, in the air, in the desert wind rising from the hot asphalt beneath our wheels. She's in the air we breathe, in my thoughts, coursing through my veins.

I tell Pigtails, "I'm thinking, even though Barstow would be a great place to hole up for the night, the town of Baker, about two hours away, looks even better right now. It has some casinos and hotels, perfect for a bit of laundering."

"Ereshkigal scares you, doesn't she? Tough guy Punchy is nervous about a woman."

I don't respond. I understand what she's doing—when feeling anxious, people often try to provoke others to distract from their own discomfort.

"This woman and her daughter that died, what were their names again?" Pigtails asks, shifting the subject.

"The woman was Jeanie. The daughter was Becky. Jeanie's death I know for sure. As for Becky... I couldn't say. My time with them, those couple of summers in Santa Cruz, was when love had been good to me." As I say this, I give Pigtails the perfect opening to criticize, but she doesn't take it.

"Becky. I like that name. You don't know what happened to Becky?" She leans over sideways, suddenly distant, pulling her hoodie over her head, perhaps replaying some nightmare in her own life. She looks like she's hiding from something.

"No," I answer into the darkened car interior. "Becky's gone, maybe changed her name, or both."

An outsider might think my words have crushed Pigtails, akin to telling her that each cigarette she smokes causes cosmic torture. I'm puzzled by her reaction—something I said clearly summoned the memory of a time her heart was broken, and I am now unsure how to ease the tension that fills the space between us.

Twelve

"Whiskey Jack's Casino?" Pigtails chuckles. "You're battling dope-sick blues, and you want to stay here? You are a walking relapse. This place is rough, dude. It's where LA folks—the skinny blonde types—stop when they can't make it home or the full jaunt to Vegas."

"Then you should fit right in," I retort. "You're as skinny as a whip. Seriously, this is the best choice right now because it's the last place on Earth you would ever pick."

"Damn straight, homie." Pigtails pauses, muttering something under her breath that I can't quite catch. Then she adds, "I see. You're so cute. The last place I would pick to hunker down is likely the last place someone would look for me."

"You pegged it, kitten."

"But we don't know where Eightball is. That motherfucker has to be in lockup—it's only been, what, ten or twelve hours since those two idiots botched their heist?"

"It's been twelve hours since their heist.

We're going to bet our brains out at the sportsbook here. Grab some cashier's checks. I'll buy them with Bobby Dynamite's ID and your cash. And we'll load you up on prepaid credit cards—I saw a liquor store that looks like they sell all kinds when we pulled in. We'll make this a decent-sized laundry stop."

"Why do you do that?"

"Do what?" I ask.

"When you talk about yourself in the third person like that, you definitely sound like you're a few veggies short of a salad or like your body isn't your own."

I let that comment slide—if she only knew.

The double-occupancy room we secure is spacious, quiet, and clean. The furniture is orange and 1970s deco. The whole place smells like a bar. Pigtails hates it here. She complains that all the shops, counters, and bars have redneck names, and the few people around make it feel haunted. She even hopes I run into Ereshkigal, my invisible friend, before the night is over. I try to laugh it off, telling her that the lack of fellow patrons is a blessing for us. "We can let our guard down a bit."

Then I tell her I need a shower to wash off the dope-sick sweat, which for some reason smells like sugar. Until today, I never knew sugar had a smell.

Pigtails tells me she wants to go downstairs to grab some bourbon and ice, informing me that the pint bottle I had earlier is long gone. This is when she throws a zinger at me. "This place does have a hokey, family-type Travelodge vibe. I bet it reminds you of going to Disneyland with Jeanie and Becky."

I try not to pause, but I do. I wrestle with the urge not to show any reaction, and at the same time, I watch her studying me with a look she's thrown my way a few times. It's as if she hears something in what I say, recognizes something, but when she tries to reconcile it with her perceptions, it doesn't align. If I were still in my Frank Montu body, would she see what she thinks she hears, and would she slowly morph deeper into the likeness of Becky?

"Disneyland? That's an odd one, girl," I fire back. "What makes you say that?"

"I don't know. Forget I said it."

"Don't be shy. Tell me what you mean."

"I don't mean anything. You must've said something earlier, and I was curious."

Pigtails is clearly holding something back. I told Ereshkigal everything—she compelled me. But to Pigtails, I've never mentioned anything about Jeanie and me taking Becky to Disneyland. I would remember if I had; pulling the scenes to the surface would have been nothing short of a knife in my chest. Disneyland was a significant chapter for Jeanie, Becky, and me—when love was truly good to me.

"I never mentioned Disneyland to—"

"Drop it, bro," Pigtails hisses. "I won't bring

it up again. You seem like the kind of dad who rolls in with big toys, amusement park trips, then disappears for days or weeks on your benders. That's all I meant."

Thirteen

The hot shower and a change into the inexpensive clothes we grabbed at Love's bring some vitality back, but Pigtails is still not back yet from her trip downstairs. It's been a while for what should have been a quick trip downstairs to grab some ice and a bottle of bourbon.

Should I be worried?

I am. That young thing, skinny as a whip, could kick my ass, but still, I worry. Even in someone else's body, I find that I can't shake the worry gene. We stopped three times on the way here. Each stop and restart, we watched for cars that stayed with us, and we played a couple of license-plate recognition games.

Nobody followed us or noticed us, as far as we could tell.

I peek out the window between the blackout blinds. It's close to midnight, and the parking lot is bustling—more cars than earlier, people coming and going in groups, cars idling.

Watching Pigtails while in Vegas is going

to be a Herculean task. Orchestrating a ruse that diverts attention toward me while Pigtails escapes to Glasgow will be as challenging as getting blood from a turnip. Like I surmised before, I won't know how to divert anybody until the first hunter makes their move. I should be used to this. In the can, predators were a dime a dozen, and they didn't exactly wear signs on their foreheads. A person's only real chance was to somehow survive the initial onslaught and then look for a way to counter.

A humbling thought dawns on me.

Pigtails left me alone in the room with her Army seabag full of cash. I could have bolted.

I could still take off.

I can't take off. What few scraps of life force and protective value I have left, I want her to have it. Every bit of it. It's more than the tenderness and vulnerability associated with innocence and youth and my daddy-fever instincts kicking in—there's something about this girl. She is special to me; she is like a daughter, yet she's not my daughter. I want her to succeed as I wanted Becky to succeed.

To steer myself away from getting too sappy, I break out the tablet and start scanning for news about the cash storage site heist. One suspect has been linked to a van fire and death—possibly Pigtails' infamous beau, Zipper. There's no mention of any other suspects or persons of interest.

Is Eightball still free? He isn't listed as an official suspect, and that's all there is to it. If he is involved, it's being kept quiet.

Pigtails and I took my car, the one I owned as Frank Montu. Nothing about Frank Montu has ever been linked to Pigtails, Zipper, or Eightball. Before we left Santa Cruz, Pigtails meticulously checked all the bank straps for trackers. She ditched her phone, and we've been using burners since Bakersfield. We should be clean, but I don't feel clean. I feel like Butch Cassidy and Sundance high in the mountains on a good run, but every time they look back, they see the posse getting closer. The posse feels like it's breathing down our necks. Am I overlooking something?

Each peek through the blinds at the parking lot below amplifies the sensation that I'm missing something crucial. Could Eightball, or anyone else, track this tablet I've been using? It was Zipper's, after all. Just to be safe, when Pigtails returns, I'll suggest we get a new tablet. Our burner flip phones are fine for texting and calling, but not for surfing the Internet or keeping an eye on the news wires. Keeping anything that belonged to the late Zipper seems like a bad idea now.

This is when the hotel room phone—an old-style landline—rings.

I walk over to the phone but don't pick it up. I let it ring.

After six rings, it stops.

I stand there trying to assess whether or

not I'm having an auditory hallucination, the kind brought on by dope sickness. The phone will ring again, I'm sure of it, like sensing a car coming down a country road before seeing it.

It does ring again!

This time, I let it ring three times before picking up. I don't say anything; I just listen. The best way to answer anything—stay quiet and listen.

"You got to get moving, babe," the voice on the other end tells me. Female. A voice from a million years ago, from a time when love was good to me. Each word stabs at my heart.

"We were a dream," I reply to Jeanie. "We were living the dream. A monster came. I wrecked it... we could've repaired and healed into something of what we had, but I would do what I did again."

"Knock it off," she answers. "You don't have time. Don't make me bring up the fact you'd been milking through the fence with some floozy the whole time we were 'building' together. By the way, how do you like our girl? She's something, isn't she?"

I stay silent, trying to connect the dots between what she's saying, what she means, and what's unfolding in front of me. Becky to Pigtails, Jeanie to this voice talking at me through the landline. It's bewildering trying to connect these dots.

"Listen to me," she continues. "Vegas was

built by people needing a place to launder money, okay? You watch any movie about money laundering—Vegas comes up at some point. You got some nasty, nasty characters wanting that money your girl has. Vegas is their first guess. Vegas is Mecca for money laundering, and you know it. Don't stay in any one spot more than a day, and always check out a couple hours before checkout time. All eyes are on the lobbies and exits at checkout time."

The hotel room door bursts open. In comes Pigtails, her eyes wide and alert, carrying a brown bag in one arm and two bags of Doritos in the other.

"You're going to have to do the ice run, dude," Pigtails tells me. "I can't do everything. I got us Jack and Doritos."

If I was in my early twenties, hanging with Pigtails would be a dream. But this battered, nearly sixty-year-old prizefighter body might not handle Doritos and Jack Daniels for a midnight snack. I try to smile, but Pigtails doesn't smile back. She looks at me like I have a penis growing out of my forehead.

"Dude, you look like the cat who swallowed the canary. I don't know who you've been trying to call. I don't want to know who you've been trying to call, but you were talking when I walked in, and that scares the crap out of me."

"I was talking," I admit.

"No shit, Sherlock. But to who?" Pigtails sets

the paper bag with the Jack on the counter and points at the floor just below the mini desk where the phone sits. "I unplugged that sonofabitch forty minutes ago, and I can see it's still unplugged. You talking to imaginary friends or something? That Ereshkigal biatch you think is after you? You calling Snuffleupagus?"

I look down, following the direction of Pigtails' pointing finger.

Oh, shit.

The phone is not plugged in. Just to double-check, I pick up the phone cradle. Nothing. No cord or cable is connected. My hamster wheel is spinning, but there's no hamster on it.

"I wasn't calling anybody," I tell her. "Just trying the phone... I got worried about you, kitten. I'm a tortoise in the shower. When you weren't back by the time I finally finished, my worry genes started talking at me."

"Okay, okay. I don't believe you. You have your burner I just bought you—you could've called me on that, homie. Maybe you prefer old-school methods and phones. That's my new nickname for you, Old School. I will only call you Punchy when it's a 911 serious thing. We can drop this topic, for now. You start tripping on me again and go cray-cray about anything, I'm out. Speaking of out, let's quit using that tablet. I will buy us a new tablet in the morning. I don't know what can or can't be tracked from that thing."

Fourteen

First thing in the morning, we check out just after 7 a.m. We find two stores that sell prepaid credit cards. I load up nine grand on one, and Pigtails does the same on another. We then swap stores to further muddy any paper trails.

Next, we hit a small Western Union where I, posing as Bobby Dynamite, wire nine grand to a location near the Glasgow airport for Pigtails. Fifteen minutes later, she wires herself the same amount to a different Western Union also close to the airport in Glasgow. Technically, she'll have ninety days to collect the money once she arrives in Glasgow. I'm hoping she'll be on a flight out of Vegas within three days.

We manage to launder fifty-four thousand dollars before breakfast—not a bad start. Our plan for the rest of the morning and midday includes using various suburbs around Vegas, like Summerlin and Henderson, for additional prepaid cards and money wiring. We'll also dip in and out of the Strip to wash larger sums at various sportsbooks.

No problems so far. No attention from strangers, no vehicles becoming real familiar.

After a half-dozen stops in the Vegas area, Pigtails buys a new tablet. I remove the SIM card from the old tablet, destroy it, and then toss the old tablet into a long-hauler with Mexico plates at the Silverton parking lot.

Next, we head to the nearest U.S. Post Office that handles emergency passports. Scanning the Glasgow obituaries, we select an elderly woman who recently passed away and use her death as the reason for Pigtails' emergency passport application.

After the post office, we strategize our next forty-eight to seventy-two hours, hoping to pick up the passport at the same location where we filed the application. However, I worry that the Feds might mistakenly send it to the address on Pigtails' driver's license—the blue door above The Tiki Room.

Our first casino stop along our revised plan is at Sam's Town, where I bet nine thousand on the 49ers to win tonight. We pause to eat Reuben sandwiches. After eating, Pigtails bets the same amount on the Niners to lose. We replicate this betting strategy at Sunset Station, except Pigtails opts for smash burgers while I skip eating. Bobby Dynamite's body isn't handling food well these days.

I'm impressed by Pigtails' intuition; she

insists we avoid main entrances and lobbies to stay under the radar. Yet all I can notice are Pigtails' features—her cheekbones, her brows, her discreet smiles. She reminds me so much of Jeanie and Becky. It's hard to focus on the dangers we face from Eightball and potentially the law. I want to protect her and ensure she gets this fresh start. I know I should focus on being vigilant, but these fatherly feelings dominate my thoughts. Eightball is coming, and law enforcement might be too. Whoever shows up will be trouble. How do I distract them long enough for Pigtails to escape with the laundered money?

I suggest to Pigtails, "We should get a different duffel bag, something square and military-looking, but not another seabag. A rucksack or a MOLLE pack. I'll carry it everywhere, making it seem like it contains the money, but you'll actually have the funds."

"That's smart," she agrees. "I was thinking something similar. It sounds like I'm setting you up to take the fall, and I hate that. But this 'driving Miss Daisy' routine has been invaluable."

"I'll carry the bag until you're safely away. We'll stash the actual funds with you—what's not already wired or shipped to Scotland. As soon as we have your passport, we buy your flight ticket. Then we FedEx your prepaid cards to whichever hotel you choose in Glasgow."

"That's the easy part. But how will you keep the attention on you while I slip away? We don't seem to have much heat on us now, but I know it's getting closer. He'll have a crew with him, no doubt. I'm getting antsy, and I see you are too."

"I wish you were my daughter," I confess. "I would buy you a car."

"In a way, you already have," she replies with a small smile. "We've been using your friend's car, and it's been a huge help. The emergency passport should be here in two days, God willing. We've already laundered more than I thought possible."

"Where are your parents?" I ask abruptly.

"That's a bit out of left field," she responds, surprised.

"I never had a real daughter. Just curious. Maybe it's some latent fatherly instinct."

"Ah. Is this more sap about that Jeanie and Becky nostalgia again? Trying to give me what you couldn't give them?"

"You don't need to be harsh," I reply, feeling a sting from her words.

"My mom passed away a long time ago," she says softly.

"What about your dad?" I probe gently.

"You're my dad right now," she answers with a furtive glance. "That's what matters. My real dad... he's probably best described as 'disappeared.'"

"What was his name?" I ask.

"I don't want to talk about it," she dismisses with finality.

Pigtails finishes her burgers, and I contemplate asking her more about her childhood —was she six, like Becky, when she lost her dad? But I decide against stirring up more of her past. We've got a good rhythm going, nearly one hundred thousand laundered, and I don't want to ignite any of her fuses.

As we walk back to the car in the Sunset Station parking garage, I actually do my job, ensuring we take a different route back. I laser beam everybody without being obvious about it, but I know I am as subtle as a chainsaw at a yoga retreat. Every passing car, every group of revelers, and every wandering eye seems suspicious.

Fifteen

That night, we hole up at a small motor lodge at the very northern edge of the Las Vegas basin. The sun has set, and everything has me jumpy. Christ, I feel like she's my kid—everything can hurt her, everything is out to get her, no matter how hard I try to protect her.

"Is this where all the scorpions live?" Pigtails asks as soon as we pull into the motor lodge parking area.

"It's the last place anyone would guess a young goddess in her mid-twenties would want to stay. It's perfect for us."

"I don't like it, but I can't disagree with you. It also kind of makes me trust you, too. In a weird way, it's almost sweet."

"I see," I tell her.

"I can tell by your voice that what I just said… the dots don't connect."

I don't say anything.

"You're really doing a smash job at trying to protect me and get me to that Glasgow-happy-ever-after scene alive. Conversely, you could be asking that we stay at the Waldorf, Hilton Resorts World, the Venetian Palazzo—something glitzy like those places—but you're really trying to keep us under the radar. You haven't even asked me for a cent. I've bought you two sandwiches and a flip phone. All the men I have met would have hounded me by now to splurge on them. Not you. An hour ago, we bought gas. I tried to pay, and your stubborn ass said otherwise. You insisted on paying and said it was Frank Montu's cookie-jar money and that it needed to go."

I'm not sure what she's getting at. I tell her, "If you are trying to thank me for being diligent, you are welcome."

"That your stoic way of warning me you are about to get more diligent?"

"The closer we get to the kitchen, the easier it gets to drop the eggs. We need to be more cautious."

"I see. And this diversion you are going to use—you know, when it's time for you and me to part—how are you going to keep the attention on you and off of me?"

Damn her. She's asking the most important question.

I don't have an answer yet. "I have a tight scenario I know will work," I tell her. "I'll share it with you when we know the passport is done, the flight is booked, and we're on our way to pick up the passport."

"Why last minute like that, Old School?"

This is a good question. If I don't answer with a real zinger, she'll think I am stalling.

I am stalling.

"Two reasons. Number one: I want to take no chances of telegraphing it to anybody who might be watching us or looking for us. If we're all jacked up about a specific plan, our body language —the way we move, things we do or don't do —gives away a lot. Only a small part of our communication is verbal; most is nonverbal. For example, you go to a job interview—that hiring manager will know whether they are going to hire you within the first minute or so, and chances are this is going to be before you've had a chance to say a word. We give away a lot, and we're not even aware of it, without even speaking."

"Fair enough. Not sure I believe you. What's the second reason you are not sharing the secret sauce of your plan until the last minute?"

"There's less chance of bungling it. I know practice makes perfect; some things need to be rehearsed. Some things... you don't rehearse them. Extracting someone's wisdom teeth. You don't rehearse that; you just do it. Rehearsing would actually be hassling. Rehearsing falling asleep at night, too. You try real hard to fall asleep, you won't. You don't try to fall asleep; you try instead to stay awake—shit, you get sleepy as hell."

"That's snake-oil wisdom, and you know it, Old School. Telling me the plan is not the same as rehearsing the plan."

"Sure, it is," I fire back. I know I'm talking out of my ass. "I have to replay the plan each time I explain it. You mentally play and replay it each time you hear it."

"Dude, you are stalling, and you're not even good at it. I have a question about the first reason for waiting until the last minute to explain your diversion plan."

"What?"

"The premise is to not share the plan with me so that we don't unconsciously telegraph anything to those who might be watching us, correct?"

"Correct."

"Okay. We drove here in Frank Montu's car that you borrowed. Zipper—God rest his soul—and Eightball know nothing about Frank Montu and his car, as far as I know. Eightball knows nothing about you, aside from what he may glean by asking questions at The Tiki Room. I'm sure you were a handy boxer, but nobody knows Bobby Dynamite. Additionally, we've got burner phones, and neither you nor I have even called anybody on them. We have a cheap-ass tablet I bought so we can use the Internet with something that is a little more efficient than our flip phones. My point is, nobody knows we're here. Who's watching us? We laundered $450k today. Tomorrow, I know we'll double that, especially if we do more sportsbook betting. Everything is rolling smooth as silk, and we did it all at the kinds of places the world has forgotten about—the mom-and-pop stores. We're not being watched, babe. I mean, I feel like we are, but it doesn't add up that we are."

"Logic. Remember logic in high school? A Happy Meal is to McDonald's what Vegas is to money laundering. Mention the phrase or the idea of 'money laundering' to anybody—the first thing to come to mind is Vegas. The idea of stolen loot brings to mind running off to Vegas. Organized crime built Vegas for this exact purpose."

Pigtails lets that one fly by. She acts like what I just told her is so nonsensical it's not even worth her breath to answer.

I don't understand these millennials. They can't admit when they have missed the mark. When I miss the mark, she'll beat that drum several times. She doesn't want to admit I am right?

Fine.

I need to know that she's well aware that Vegas is the first place even a dumbass like Eightball is going to look for her. I know she knows this, but it will make me feel good seeing her be redundant in admitting it's a safe bet that Eightball is here, and he is close.

We unload the car. Secure ourselves in the tiny room. She showers and cleans up first. I watch TV without the volume and peek out the gap in the curtains intermittently. I know she feels like we are being hunted but doesn't think we are in danger. I know we have company in Vegas looking for Pigtails so they can punch her ticket.

This room is rough, but I actually feel a little bit safe. I need a good night's sleep tonight—not just because I want this dope-sick stuff to be gone. We have a grinder of a day coming up. Tomorrow, we are going to hit a ton of sportsbooks—our chance for football bets. We can only launder $18k per sportsbook: nine from a bet placed by me that a team wins, and nine from Pigtails that the same team loses. I suspect we'll be using some of the sportsbook places on the Strip. I'm a little nervous about that because we have to visit each place twice—once to bet, once to collect.

Unless we want to hang out. Sitting still is a bad idea.

Pigtails comes out of the bathroom in sweats and a hoodie. She gives me a brief nod that it's my turn. I grab what few supplies I have and go into the bathroom. I take the shower as hot as it will deliver. Burn off the last of my dope-sick fever. I shave and brush my teeth. This is when my little flip phone chirps.

A text from Pigtails.

**PIGTAILS:
Somebody just
knocked on the
door. WTF!! Three
times. Hard.
Maybe you heard
it. I didn't answer.
I shut off all the**

lights in case the creep tries to peek in somehow. Make sure the light is off before you open the bathroom door and come out. Please hurry up.

I knew this was coming—a touch from a tentacle belonging to one of the underworld monsters looking for us.

How I respond is much more important than what I respond with. I certainly do not want to respond with reaction. I need to be slow and quiet, observe everything.

The first thing I do is lock the bathroom door. The second thing I do is put my flip phone on vibrate. I follow this by gently sliding the narrow, up-high bathroom window closed and making sure the lock catches. Then I put my toothbrush and toothpaste back in my bag. Fix my pants and my shirt. I stow my bag of toiletries beneath the sink. I grab the phone and turn off the bathroom light. Gently as possible, I place my ear against the door and listen while letting my eyes adjust to the dark.

Nothing.

I reach for the knob, unlock it. More listening.

Nothing.

I turn the knob and pull the door open. Slow

and steady, I inch forward while staying crouched.

Pigtails is right there on the other side, waiting for me to do what I just did.

Using slow and big hand gestures, I signal for Pigtails to switch places with me.

She squeezes past me and enters the bathroom. I exit the bathroom.

We pause while passing each other so she can whisper at me. "There was the knock. I paused, then I hit the lights. I inched up to the peephole. There's nobody there. I moved over to the big window and looked out through the gap in the drapes. All I see are two cars out there—beaters, you know, like rental cars. Both have their lights on, aimed at our room and the room next door. Some dude out there standing between the cars like he belongs to one car and is talking to whoever is inside the other car."

I nod, and then I crawl into the main room.

I hear the bathroom door shut behind me and the doorknob lock click into place. I take a deep breath and continue crawling up to the entrance door of our motel room. I rise slowly until I can see out the peephole. I can smell cigarette smoke. Whoever's on the other side is having a ciggie.

I do not see anybody.

Okay. Ciggie-face is being a sneak, purposely standing outside of the peephole view.

I squat back down and crawl over to the right and look through the gap in the drapes.

There's only one car out there now. I can't

tell the make, but she was right. Some rental-car beater thing you get at the airport. The lights are on and aimed right at our room. The cigarette smoke I smell is absolutely from someone on the other side of our door—that car out there with the lights on and the engine running is too far away.

I text Pigtails to hold tight. Five more minutes.

And I am dead-on correct.

It takes less than five minutes, and the idling car leaves.

Cigarette man?

I am not sure where that cat went.

Pigtails creeps back out of the bathroom. She takes one twin bed. I take the other. I fix us both a lowball glass with Jameson and a little ice. It's not that bad like this in the dark. The only light is what comes through the gap in the drapes. What little bit of illumination is comparable to the help I might provide to Pigtails in this banged-up Bobby Dynamite rig: broken streams and dim and —hopefully—enough.

We both agree to just stay like this a while, see if our visitor comes back.

Sixteen

Bobby Dynamite's body may like heroin, but it sure isn't receptive to whiskey so much. I wake with a bit of a hangover, same as yesterday, having only had about three or four sips of whiskey. No problem for me—I'd rather get lit from three shots as opposed to eight.

We scram early, on the road by 7 a.m. Neither of us mentions the night before and the accompanying door knock. First, we hit a dozen mom-and-pop stores and do the prepaid-card thing. Then we go to breakfast at the illustrious Bellagio. There is a buffet that is famous, and Pigtails insists.

While at the Bellagio, we bet nine grand apiece at one of the sportsbooks. I don't like it. There are waves and eddies of people, swarms flowing around us—running right through us if they could. Everybody is watching us. Pigtails insists we go next door to Caesars to bet at their sportsbook. I try to remind her that we'll have to come back to both of these places to collect our money, which are the most popular places, increasing our risk. She gives me the back of her hand and calls me a boomer. Bobby Dynamite, according to his expired boxing licenses and his suspended driver's license, was born in 1966. So I'm a Gen-Xer—an early Gen-Xer. I don't say anything—I'd rather be happy than be right.

After Caesars, she drags me across the street to the Venetian. We hit two more sportsbooks while over there.

"I'm glad you don't have kids, and I bet you are, too," Pigtails tells me.

"That's a weird thing to say. Especially the day after I sincerely expressed wishing you were my daughter—how I'd buy you a car and spoil you."

"Jeez. Shush. Sometimes you are like a Democrat... every little thing offends. What I'm saying is kind of agreeing—you're letting me get away with... whatever. If you had a daughter, you would have ruined that girl. Made her into a total daddy's-little-princess."

"I'm glad you see that," I fire back. "We need to get out of here. I've had goosebumps for the last twenty minutes."

"You are being paranoid."

"Look, you are adorable. I'd be proud if you were my daughter. But you got gumball-blue hair in pigtails, and everybody who's looking for us knows you as Pigtails. You took the pants we bought at Love's and cut the legs off so they are now mini-mini shorts. Combat boots. You're wearing a tube top so everybody can see your ten-thousand tattoos. And you got fishing-tackle stuff in your nose, lips, and ears."

"What are you saying, Old School? You embarrassed to be around me?"

"I am proud as hell to be with you, but we stick out like a broken nose, girl."

She stops walking. Stares at me with her hands on her hips. "One more big casino here on the Strip, okay? Then we can go back to lurking on the outskirts—you vibe better on the lower rungs; we can do the lower rungs."

I don't say anything. I just nod.

The final casino we visit on the Strip is the Aria. Crazy. If anybody is following us, watching us, looking extra hard at us, I won't see it. We are in a flowing soup of people, thick as any starling murmuration.

We bet at a sportsbook, nine grand each. Then we head back to the car. And this is when things get screwy again.

To walk from Aria to Bellagio, we pass through the lobby of Vdara, a spacious, quaint hotel. Nice lobby, and nice restrooms, which is why we stop.

I wait outside the women's room in the marbled hallway while Pigtails uses the restroom. I do not notice the man until he has gently sidled up beside me. So quiet and elegant. No shorter than six-two, lean build. Dust-bowl lean, lots of ropy muscle, plenty of veins standing out in the arms and neck. He has a big, big smile, and he's aiming it right at me like I got horns growing out of my head. Back in the can, warning him to quit eye-fucking me is the right response.

Nowadays, I have been using a softer script.

I nod, smile, and continue to mind my own business—on the outside, that is. On the inside, I am trying to read him, vibe out the weak spot. I know he's about to say something, and I need to answer back, but I have to answer back with nothing. I can't ignore him; that's disrespect. I can't freeze up, either. You freeze up, he'll think he's got me. I played this game plenty at Pelican Bay.

"The Strip these days," he tells me. He puts a little laugh behind his voice. "This place is like Disneyland for adults. And the gaming is amazing. You coming out ahead?" he asks. He hands me what looks like a piece of chewing gum as he asks this last part.

I look at the gum, shake my head no. Then I look him directly in the eyes—like he raped and killed my mother. I look into his pupils like I can see into his head and out the back. What I see there scares me. I can feel the warmth in my body drain out through my feet, similar to how I felt when I met with Ereshkigal. What gives me the biggest creeps is the gum he tried to hand me. It's Juicy Fruit. I can smell it. The dude's coming at me with sweetness, but what he'll deliver is poison.

No doubt, I gotta get this guy to pack sand

before Pigtails comes out of the head.

"You'll get better conversation out of someone else," I tell him. I try to say it as flat-out as possible. He breaks the pupil stare first, much to my relief, looks down at his gum, and says, "I beg to differ. See, you look real familiar to me." And then, after a pause, and with the utmost confidence, he adds, "I know I know you."

"A lot of people tell me that," I answer back. "You and I, however, can agree to disagree. I don't know you." The whole time I am telling him this, I notice his cauliflower ears. The scarred brows. This cat's a brawler.

"We'll see," he answers back softly. "Maybe we'll find out you're wrong…" He doesn't finish. He doesn't get a chance. Goddamn Pigtails walks out of the head, stinking like some kind of patchouli thing, and steps right up beside me and grabs onto my arm like she's drowning and my nearly sixty-year-old, collapsed-veins limb is the last flotation device on Earth.

"Who are you?" she asks, wagging her chin at the tall man. She says it crisply.

"I'm just saying hello," he answers softly. "Your father here looked familiar, that's all. You do, too. You look really familiar—the star of the show. A superstar."

"I'm not familiar," she sasses right back. Then, nodding her head in my direction, she tells the tall man, "This beautiful man I'm hanging onto is my freak on the side. He doesn't know you because I don't know you. The way I dress, which is my choice, turns weak men into stalkers. Are you weak, are you going to be a problem?"

The tall man looks right at me when he answers Pigtails. "Hang in there, captain. I'm sure I'll be seeing you. Seeing you up close. We are going to finish our conversation. I can't speak for you, but I know I am a finisher."

And then he walks off in long strides.

Seventeen

"That was the devil," Pigtails snaps at me. She's digging through the glove box, looking for the cigarettes we stashed in there on the first day, like she's a giant marmot digging for food. We are back at Frank Montu's car in the Bellagio parking garage.

I wish I could agree with her. I want the tall man to be similar to Ereshkigal: nebulous, someone I suspect is a hallucination. Snuffleupagus.

But the tall man was very real, and I know he is going to be a very real problem.

"That was no devil, babe," I tell her. "Something worse. Somebody who makes any previous notions of Satan silly by contrast. He's exactly who I will be leading on a chase while you scramble off to Scotland."

"Don't be an asshole," she answers back. "I told you I don't like you being the fall guy. You keep pushing my guilt triggers. I said yes to your offers when you brought up the Driving Miss Daisy part, but there's nothing good-feeling about imagining myself leaving you behind to deal with that freak show and Eightball and anyone else."

"You're right. I will be more careful with my words. The good thing is, we have a glimpse of who might be a problem."

She finds the cigarettes and lights two of them. She hands one to me. I climb into the driver's side, start the car.

"I thought the rule was no smoking in the car?"

"You thought correct. That hasn't stopped you before. Besides, I gotta get us out of here. I feel trapped in the parking garage. I will break the rule this once."

"That fuckface we just dealt with—is he the doorknocker guy from last night?" she asks.

"I doubt it. That cat last night smokes. Smokes a lot. The tall man today—I don't know what he is, but he's the Boss of Gum. Motherfucker smelled like Juicy Fruit."

"I hate this. Every time you start thinking heavy, you get quiet, you answer basic questions with riddles or half-answers, and you shut me out. Boss of Gum? Juicy Fruit? For the record, I hate Juicy Fruit."

"Look, kitten, we gotta come back to the Strip tonight, or maybe crack of dawn, and collect your winnings. You want to know what worries me? That worries me."

"That's fine. Set a room call to wake us up,

collect everything at three in the morning. Should be safe."

I don't answer at first. Then I tell her, "There's plenty we can get done on the 'outskirts,' as you call it. Prepaid cards. Sportsbooks. We haven't done any Western Union today."

"Dude, can we just chill a few minutes? Boss of Gum was scary for me."

"You really handled him superbly," I tell her. "I couldn't be more proud of you. I stood there frozen, even after all my time in the joint, and you played that scenario perfectly."

"When that passport comes in tomorrow, like they quoted us—cross your fingers—I need to book my ticket, pick a Glasgow hotel, make reservations, FedEx my prepaid cards... there's a lot of them. Maybe not so heavy on the Western Union stuff. Each time we wire something, that's one more place for me to visit, another chore, if and when I get to Glasgow."

"You'll get to Glasgow," I tell her. "And you're right, we have a chore list from hell hanging over our heads."

To vent out our fear from the Boss of Gum, we do the opposite of what she suggested—we go on a crazy rampage of Western Union locations. At each location, we each wire nine grand to Pigtails Brokaw. Each wiring goes to a different Western Union in Glasgow. According to Exchange Finder, there are thirty-one Western Union locations in Glasgow. Pigtails and I finish sending nine grand each to every single Western Union in Glasgow by three in the afternoon.

Inside, I am laughing. Her first few weeks in Glasgow, she'll be spending all her time visiting Western Union offices. She'll be buzzing around like she has a job instead of partying it up like any twenty-two-year-old would do.

Our next stops are the casinos on the outskirts of Las Vegas—the small casinos where locals gamble. Most of the places have a shitkicker vibe. Honky-tonks. I feel safer. We have time to brace a dozen sportsbooks. I like the honky-tonks, and I don't know why this is, but I feel like the Boss of Gum doesn't fit well in honky-tonks. This doesn't make any sense because the dude is tall, lean, and ropy strong. He's got the perfect cowboy physique.

Toward sunset, we find a hotel on the opposite side of the Las Vegas basin from our first night in Vegas.

The Sleep Tight Lodge.

"Last night we stayed where scorpions are born. Tonight, you want to stay where tarantulas are born."

"You know the reason," I answer back.

"It didn't work so well last night."

"How do you know?" I fire back.

She's right, of course. I'm not used to feeling defensive, but I am feeling defensive, which probably means I really do care about this young lady—I care about her well-being, and I want her to get that new start in Scotland.

"The doorknocker—we don't know that he was the Boss of Gum. I smelled cigarettes, not gum. The guy today? He smelled like gum."

"When I peeked out the drapes, I saw two cars idling, lights aimed at our room. Somebody was standing between the two cars, talking between the two cars. How do you know that wasn't the Boss of Gum?"

"Look, kid, people travel in groups. We don't know it had anything to do with Eightball."

"That is a bogus politician kind of answer. You gonna look, or do I need to look?" she asks.

"Look for what?"

"You boomers. You're lost half the time. Go on the tablet, scope out Eightball's socials— especially LinkedIn and Facebook—and look for pics of the freak show we met today at Vdara. The Boss of Gum—look for pics of his sorry ass."

"How about we both do it? I do it first, then you."

"That's another boomer trait," she sasses at me. "Repeat stuff. Do stuff multiple times."

"Technically, I'm fifty-nine. 1966. Generation X."

"Yeah. That's what I'm saying. You Gen Xers are boomers part deux."

Eighteen

I come out of the shower. Pigtails is sitting on the floor in the half-lotus position.

"What did you find?" I ask.

"Jack shit is what I found about the Boss of Gum. There are no pics of that demon on any of Eightball's socials. You can look if you want, if your boomer Gen Xer tendencies need their redundancy fix. No posts or anything on any of the newswires about Eightball. I checked the ass-blotter for Santa Cruz County and Santa Clara County. When Zipper went down, Eightball skated."

Her voice wobbles when she says this last part. It's obvious Zipper is a subject she'll do her best to avoid until Scotland. I know she doesn't want me to see her hurt for loving a man who was terrible and ran with terrible people.

"Then Eightball never made it past the 'person of interest' level of importance," I add.

"Eightball and Daddy have great lawyers," Pigtails replies.

"He's here. Eightball, I mean. Let's just assume he's here, and he's got a crew. Boss of Gum —shit, hopefully he was a random psychopath. Nothing more."

"We've laundered everything down to 180K. That passport comes in tomorrow, I'm out. Do you want to share your secret plan for diverting attention off me once I have that ticket and I'm getting through the airport gates safely? This last-minute enough? You know I need to know because there's nothing that feels good about you falling on your sword so I can get away."

"Tomorrow morning, at the ass-crack of dawn—start in the wee hours—we hit all the sportsbooks, grab your wins. Then we stay away from casinos by focusing on the prepaid cards. Buy up 180K worth. Twenty more at nine grand a pop will do it—close enough. That being complete, we FedEx the whole lot of cards to whatever place you know you'll be at when you get to Glasgow. After that, we hole up where nobody will look until your flight comes in."

"What about the other part?" she asks. "I was asking about the other part."

"What other part?"

"I just told you. The part that hurts me. The part where you go one direction and draw all the attention. I go the other direction—hopefully unnoticed."

"When you have that passport in hand, flight booked, I'll spill it. I'm glad you asked because I need something from you."

"What?"

"Tomorrow morning, when it's sunny out, I need to get a picture of you. Cutoffs, tube top, combat boots, blue pigtails, all that. How you look being you is what I need to capture."

"Don't get weird on me now, Old School. This is how I always dress."

I don't say anything.

"I get it," she assures me. "You need it for some crazy reason that's connected to our 'exit strategy,' your top-secret diversion plan."

"The other thing I want to do," I tell her, "the big casino sportsbooks we can collect anytime. I think we should go between 3 a.m. and 6 a.m. Go to the smaller ones as soon as they open."

"You saying we should go to sleep right now, be up by three?"

"Something like that."

"I'm not tired. We need to be up at three—I won't sleep."

"Then I suggest we stay off the booze—at least pretend to rest. Worst case, we'll be tired but sober instead of tired and hangdog."

"Shit, boo, speak for yourself. I can handle my booze."

We agree to keep the lights off, the curtains drawn shut. The TV is on, and so are the closed captions. The room is dead quiet.

It turns out Pigtails can handle her booze just fine—handles the booze by not handling it.

That girl was zonked out before I had a chance to scoot out to the car and grab our bottle of Jameson. The full day really wiped her out.

I sit in the dark and watch the TV screen. Some show where lions are fighting hippos and crocs and water buffalo. The Serengeti. I feel sad. My whole life has been like that. *Mission Impossible.* And I have been the worst enemy to myself that I could possibly meet.

Out of the corner of my eye, I can see into the bathroom. There is movement in there.

The room is suddenly cold. Ice cold. I can see my breath.

The bathroom lights are off, aside from what faded blue flickers from the TV reach that far, but I can see half of the mirror above the bathroom sink. Jeanie is in there, watching the mirror, watching me, and fixing her hair.

I take one last look at Pigtails.

Homegirl is still comatose.

I stand from my twin bed gently and quietly. I walk to the tiny bathroom, go inside, and shut the door.

I am not frightened. My mind is clear: void of judgment, opinion, and comparison. Void of alcohol fog and DTs. This makes me wonder if those who are blessed with mediumistic abilities are simply humans who ride the imaginative flow instead of using judgment, opinion, and comparison to separate this from that. Nonetheless, I have missed Jeanie more than I can quantify to the all-knowing darkness.

Jeanie murmurs something unintelligible at me.

My intuition tells me to leave the light off. Keep it dark—this'll make it easier for me to hear and feel and see Jeanie. The rational part of me thinks my roof isn't nailed down so tight. Both hemispheres of my mind are always at war, whether I had the Frank Montu body or here in the Bobby Dynamite body.

"I'm real proud of her," Jeanie tells me. Her voice is a sultry whisper. "I know you are, too, babe. You've done great keeping her on track. Anyone else would've ripped her off the first moment she dropped her guard."

"She did great," I add. "You should have seen her handle the Boss of Gum. I froze up like a fresh fish on the yard."

"Don't joke around with that one, the Boss of Gum," Jeanie hisses. "He's one of three thorns in your side. He's the biggest thorn, and it's a thorn steeped in poison."

"You want to help me out with that?" I ask. I can hear my voice rising and try to tone it down.

Jeanie tells me, "You know what he is. He's a fixer. Don't drop your hands. You are a mystery to him right now; otherwise, he would have pounced. As soon as he thinks he has a read on you—or you have all that swag laundered—watch out!"

"Look, babe, you know what I'm asking. What're the other two thorns?"

"The obvious is Eightball, and he is connected to Gum."

"Copy that. Who's the third thorn?"

"It's more of a what than a who."

I wait. It's what she wants. She thinks the next piece of information she gives me will be rhetorical—an answer we both know is true and that I've been dodging.

"You killed Seifert, and I know you would do it again in similar circumstances. A monster he was. We lost you but would've been able to visit you. The big blow was learning you'd been milking through the fence. You were cheating the whole time we had our happy little home."

"Is that what this is about tonight, to torture me? I'm real close to getting that young lady on a plane, provided I can keep the baddies looking in a different direction. You show up now to drown me in shame. If you're trying to throw me off, you won't. I got nothing to lose. That girl in the other room is getting her win. I will see to that."

"I'm not drowning you. You may or may not get that girl out of here alive, but you will be seeing Ereshkigal again—your third thorn. Forgiveness leads to acceptance. Acceptance leads to understanding. Understanding leads to appreciation. Appreciation is the closest neighbor to unconditional love—where we all come from. Ereshkigal will find you where you are at, whether it's shame and judgment or appreciation. You need to pick your poison, tough guy. Your way out is to go in."

Forgiveness. *Fuck forgiveness,* I want to scream at Jeanie. My life has been life on the Serengeti right out of the gate. There've been zero easy days.

This is when loud knocking on the bathroom door breaks my fugue state.

Pigtails.

"Old School? You going cuckoo on me? Don't be tripping on me now, asshole!" Pigtails is banging on the door as she yells.

"You going to help me or not?" I ask Jeanie.

"Your exit… of course I will help," Jeanie barks with a laugh. "You need a fugazi. A double."

"I've been working on that part," I fire back.

"You need to hurry. Plenty of things to watch out for tomorrow."

"Hey, cut that shit out," Pigtails yells through the door after knocking again. "You're talking to yourself, and it's scaring me, Punchy."

Christ. She only calls me Punchy when it's DEFCON-level serious.

"Be out in a minute. Don't act like you don't talk to yourself," I yell back to Pigtails.

"Yes. But you are talking and then answering back to yourself. Sounds scary as shit."

I don't say anything. I look for Jeanie.

Jeanie's gone. She's not in the bathroom with me, and she's not in the mirror. The only thing in the mirror is me, inside a Bobby Dynamite body that has had its day.

Pigtails again: "Hurry up, Old School, I need to pee."

Nineteen

T he phone wake-up call is right on time: 2:45 a.m. No problem. I am already awake. Pigtails is comatose. She'll stay that way until I wake her. Waking Pigtails is a bit of a project, much like giving a cat a pill.

I don't know how it is when she sleeps late —perhaps she's sweet as an apple. We haven't had that chance. Each day since leaving Santa Cruz, we have been up early, and she wakes on the wrong side of the snake nest.

Quietly, I go into the bathroom to scrub my fangs, wash my face, and look through my secret little book. Yesterday, during our many stops, I managed to grab a small, color-printed escort directory called *Happy Endings*. I did it on the sly, as I know Pigtails would have a Chernobyl-level meltdown and probably kill me or cripple me if she'd seen me grab it.

I page through the book and choose four different providers who have Pigtails' height and build and specialize in cosplay. It seems all the men and women in the magazine specialize in cosplay. I tear the pages out showing the schedules and contact information of each of the providers that check the boxes I want checked. I tuck the folded pages into my back pocket. Then I shove the rest of the book under the sink, wedged between the pipe and the wall.

Plausible deniability. If Pigtails somehow finds the escort directory, I don't know where it came from. Someone before us must have left it here.

It's too early to expect coffee to be made at the hotel lobby, and I do not want to be seen going in and out of the room multiple times. I'm still spooked from the after-hours door-knock scene the night before and the Mr. Gum nightmare at Vdara. My Jeanie experience made the Gum-and-Eightball connection clear as day.

What I do is make coffee as best I can here in the hotel room. Christ, I'm making it in the bathroom sink.

I make four strong cups—two for me and two for Pigtails. I leave two cups in the bathroom and take my two cups out. I give Pigtails a gentle but sturdy shake, let her know where two strong cups of coffee are waiting for her in the bathroom. This is the only way I can get her to move. She does move. And when she's in the head, the shower loudly running, I bring out my escort pages from my back pocket and give them another once-over.

Somewhere along the way today, I need to

look at these more closely, talk to each provider voice-to-voice, and make my choice. Pigtails and I have a busy day today, and given the scenes with the door knocker and Mr. Gum, I will be holding Pigtails close to me. Connecting with the escorts I've picked out will be a clandestine task of misdirection that would be difficult even for Houdini.

I put the papers back in my pocket, pack what few things I have, and stack my stuff next to the door. My ideal scene is to do one trip from door to car, lessening our time out in the open.

Pigtails finishes her shower and comes out bouncing around, dressed the way she always dresses, which is what I will need a picture of as soon as it is sunny out. Yesterday I told her I was going to get a pic of her dressed the way she normally does as soon as the sun came out, and I meant that. I need a clean shot of her.

"You're bright-eyed and bushy-tailed," I tell her.

"Bet your old ass I am. Had a dream that text comes through around three in the afternoon letting me know the passport is waiting for me."

"I got that feeling, too," I tell her. "From noon onward, we'll try to stay near the passport pickup spot. When you get that text, we won't miss it."

"Our plan the same as last night?" she asks.

"We go to the big casino sportsbooks as soon as you're ready. Grab your payouts. Then we'll go to the smaller ones when they open. You know we're going to be running hot today. No downtime. After we collect the sportsbook winnings, we stay away from the casinos and stick to grabbing up $180K worth of prepaid cards."

"Once I have that passport and book the flight, what then?"

"We FedEx the prepaid cards to where you think you'll be staying in Glasgow. Then I take you straight to the airport."

"What if, say, I book the flight, we send the FedEx package, and there's still twenty hours or some crazy time cushion before my flight?"

"I'm still taking you to the airport. I already checked. At Harry Reid Airport, you can go through security up to 24 hours before your flight. You will be safer on the other side of the security gate than you will be with me. Worst-case scenario, you'll have to wait a few hours sitting at an overpriced bar."

"Damn, boo. You've been ten steps ahead the whole time. The man with all the answers."

"I want you to have this win," I tell her. "I want you to have a fresh start in Glasgow—no more Eightballs, no more Zippers. You get a page-one beginning with plenty of cash to keep you safe."

Pigtails lunges forward, hugs me, and then backs off a bit.

"I'm glad I'm not your daughter. Even being a stranger, it's going to hurt like a sonofabitch when you drop me off at the airport."

"We need to go," I tell her.

Pigtails gathers her things. We turn on all the lights, give the room a final once-over, and then we leave.

Outside, I can smell sage. The air is crisp and dry. It is still dark. Normally, looking up at the endless starry skies soothes me, and looking at any kind of horizon meeting the stars is icing on the cake.

Not this pre-dawn.

It's so odd. The Toyota that belongs to Frank Montu—the old me—has been running great. Not a problem, great on gas, but it has gotten dusty. As I load our few things into the trunk and backseat, Pigtails points at the rear window. Someone drew a large frowny face in the dust. And below the frowny face, they wrote:

"I'll B Seeing U."

"What is that?" I ask. I know what it is.

"What's it look like?" Pigtails sasses back.

"Someone wrote on my window dust."

"You know who."

"You thinking Gum did?" I ask. I know the answer, and she's right.

"Last thing that motherfucker said to you was something about 'I'll be seeing you.' Look at your window, homie."

I walk the circumference of the car. I don't know what I am looking for. This is when I see it.

A chewed piece of gum spat out onto the

ground, and right next to it, the wrapper from its replacement. The paper wrapper dropped so recently it hasn't had a chance to blow away.

I pick up the wrapper and smell it.

Goddamn Juicy Fruit.

"How?" she hisses at me from across the car.

"I don't know, babe."

"It couldn't have been him. Why didn't he kick the door in, strong-arm what little bit of cash I got left, drag me away, and hand me to Eightball?"

That's a damn good question.

I look around—left, right—stare long at the office. I look behind us. I don't feel like we're being watched, but I know Gum rolled through. Plenty of working cameras spaced evenly along the roof gutters—each with a little red light indicating it's on.

"Too many cameras," I tell her. "Beyond that, I couldn't say why he held off doing more than writing on my ride. He must've followed us from the Bellagio."

"Wrong. Wrong. I know that fucker is the one who banged on our door at the other place. He was following us before the Bellagio. And I know exactly why he hasn't done the smash-and-grab where he drags me and the money off to Eightball... yet. The operative word is *yet*."

"I want to hear what you think," I tell her. I bet she does know. These millennials are ten steps ahead most of the time.

These pitched and intense thoughts of

being followed remind me of something I almost conveniently forgot.

Something that will likely be an added problem.

My Frank Montu body is certainly swollen and smelling awful by now—the aroma being big enough to be detected regardless of the crazy neighbor who cooks bacon every day. Someone will do a welfare check. The car belonging to Frank Montu is gone. Did someone murder him? Maybe an APB will be put out on the car I'm driving with Bobby Dynamite's suspended license.

Certainly something to consider.

Twenty

It's a quarter to nine in the hot Vegas morning—the dynamic duo have been up for hours, and the day is just starting. We've just collected all Pigtails' winnings from the big casinos on the Strip. We'll collect from the smaller casinos next and then buy as many prepaid credit cards as there are mom-and-pop stores we can find. Once it gets close to noon, I want to stay near the location from which we hope to pick up Pigtails' passport as soon as she gets that text.

I should be happy.

I'm not.

There is a crazy-ass buffet thing going down at Caesars.

We're in line.

The buffet opens in ten minutes. I have too many red flags cracking off right now. Everybody is watching us. Not like I'm her dad or we're some May-and-December matchup. We're getting looks like we're science projects, space aliens.

Additionally, there's only one casino

between Caesars and Vdara—where we saw Gum.

Not enough space for me.

I want as much space as possible from anything that reminds me of Gum or Eightball, especially this close to the finish line. Caesars is tied for the title of the most popular OG of casinos, and the buffet here is a celebrity in its own right. All this has me itching like a man on a fuzzy tree.

Not to mention, that first night at Whiskey Jack's, Jeanie told me to stay away from the big casinos at checkout time. Eleven a.m. is checkout time.

Pigtails, reading my mind and my worry genes again, tells me, "Shit, homeboy didn't kick in the door and drag me off last night for the same reason they didn't do it the night they banged on the motor lodge door."

"You keep saying that. Are you ever going to share why you think that?" I ask.

"What was the name of that movie where that dude rolls into a medieval Japan harbor on a boat? Handsome cat gets shipwrecked there or something."

"*Shōgun*," I answer with a laugh. "How does that have anything to do with Gum?"

"The round-eye shows up in Japan, has ship problems. They could've wiped him out on sight, all those goddamn archers. They didn't because he was an anomaly—an X-factor. That's you, bro. You show up right when I bolted with a lot of money Eightball thinks is his, and you have a face that looks like you stopped a train with it..."

"Excuse me?" I interrupt.

"Don't flatter your self-loathing self on my behalf. I'm not saying you're ugly, but you've seen some battles, and you look like you've seen battles. This makes you a spooky unknown."

"If you're correct—and I know you are," I tell her, "as soon as they feel like they have a clean read on me, they'll pounce."

This is also something Jeanie told me when I was talking to myself and the darkness in the bathroom.

"Bang on correct, which will likely be today, depending on how much they see you and read into what they see. My bet: they will start really circling the drain in tighter and tighter circles as soon as I've collected all my winnings."

"Sure," I add. I'm only chiming along to self-soothe by hearing myself talk. "They don't know the details, but they know you've been laundering through the casinos. Before dark, they'll rush in and grab you."

Pigtails nods.

"Then why are we right here, next door to the casino that's next door to our last Gum experience?" I snap. "Why are we out in the open making it easy for anyone watching to assess what kind of a threat I am?"

"Because I want this. Just one luxury meal in Vegas—one archetypal Vegas moment. Can't even imagine how long I'll be a Glasgow girl."

"Fine. A last hoorah!"

"I also want to do one more stop here at Caesars. Get myself a fine outfit. Just one. Something sleek and elegant."

I don't say anything. She's going to get us killed is how I feel. I have some cheap shades on so I can scan the whole dining area and not look like I'm scanning.

I don't see anyone being too grandiose about X-raying Pigtails and myself.

The line moves forward, and we're finally given a seat. It's a decent spot where I can have my back against the wall and laser-beam most of the dining area.

I still don't see anybody working too hard to eyeball us.

I tell Pigtails I'm going to the head.

The walk to the restroom is easy. I pick the last stall in the far back corner. I pull out my pages from the escort directory. On my little flip phone, I type out a message, copy it, and then text each of the four escorts I had picked out. What I text is just a simple checklist of what I want and, of course, the bonus I'll pay if they can do it today.

Then I spend the next ten minutes trying to make sure all the ringtones are off on this phone. If I go back to the table and have this phone beeping or vibrating, Pigtails will knock my block off.

The first reply from an escort rolls through just as I'm about to leave the stall, but I don't have a chance to scope it out. The restroom I'm in is long and marbled and empty. So when the tall, lumbering character in cowboy boots walks in and slowly walks past all the empty stalls except for the one next to the stall I'm sitting in, my worry genes start chirping at me. Although I can't see through the stall walls, I know this man is tall by the space between his bootfalls—the long stride.

What I also don't like—this dude is whistling the *Bridge on the River Kwai* song, the creepy, haunting bastard.

I fold the phone and stash it in my shirt pocket. I stand and exit the stall. I don't flush, don't wash my hands—I just leave.

The whistling sounds stay with me until I am completely out of the restroom.

Big, big relief floods all through me when I see Pigtails piling all manner of things on her plate at the seafood section.

I return to my seat, grab my coffee, and watch the bathroom entrance. I need to see who that was that went in there while I was in there. Mr. Slow Walk trying to scare my ass—and I need to see him. Ten empty stalls, and the dude picked the one next to the stall I was in. If he looks directly at me or Pigtails when he comes out, we have a problem.

Nobody with cowboy boots exits.

I wait some more.

Nobody with cowboy boots exits.

I keep watching.

Pigtails returns to the table. Her plate is as

full as a plate can get, shrimp and things hanging off the sides. Even her cheeks are full, similar to how hamsters store nuts.

I keep watching the men's room exit, but nobody's coming out.

"Where's your mind at, homeboy?" she asks me. "You went to the bathroom for at least twenty minutes. I was worried you fell in or something. And now you're watching the doorway like you've seen a ghost."

"I locked myself in the stall farthest back. No other stalls were being used. Some cat in boots strolls in real slow, skips all the other stalls except the one next to mine."

"Creepy, man. Damn. What kind of boots?"

"Pointy-toed shitkicker boots. Cowboy boots, basically."

"I see," Pigtails adds. "You don't know what he looks like, but you could at least see boots under the stall, so you're waiting for boots to come out."

"Bingo."

Pigtails eats and watches the restroom entrance with me.

No boots.

"Aren't you hungry?" she asks with a mouth full of food. "We've been up for hours."

"I'll go in a minute."

"Go now. I'll watch for Mr. Boots." Then, after a pause, she tells me, "Come on, man, you've been back at least five minutes. That dude slipped out while you blinked."

"The hell he did," I tell her and stand from my seat. "Give me five minutes."

I walk briskly but casually back to the men's room. I still feel like everyone and their brothers, sisters, cousins, and neighbors are watching Pigtails and myself.

Inside the men's room.

Nothing.

There's a man helping a youngster wash his hands.

I walk all the way down to the last stall and back out again. No cowboy boots.

I want to check for messages from the escorts, but I can't. Pigtails is watching the restroom entrance. If I take too much time leaving the restroom, she'll worry and be suspicious.

I get back to the table. Pigtails' plate is empty, her napkin is on the table, her arms are crossed, and she gives me a fierce stink eye as soon as I sit.

"Just as I thought," she tells me. "Another goddamn ghost. One of your invisible friends."

"That was no ghost. Somehow, he slipped out when I blinked, that's all."

"Dude, just this last night you were talking to yourself and answering back. That first night we drove here, remember, you were talking on a phone that wasn't plugged in. You have some glitches in your matrix where you talk to spooks."

"What kind of bathing suit are you getting?" I ask. I need to change the subject away from seeing things and ghosts. I know that dude with cowboy boots was real. Besides, every time she mentions ghosts, I think of Ereshkigal—a nightmare I've been able to stuff into a closet and keep packed away there.

"Bathing suit?"

"Yeah. You just told me a few minutes ago you wanted to hit a few shops here at Caesars and get a bathing suit for Scotland."

"Bathing suit? Shit, Glasgow is colder than a well digger's ass. I am definitely getting something slinky, but no bathing suits. You're trying to change the subject."

"Change the subject from what?"

"You don't want to admit you have some glitches. I sure have glitches. What was I doing with Zipper? I get a couple days of distance from that whole scene, and I'm thinking, who was that, that's not me? Skateboards, ashtrays, empty beer bottles—we lived in a dump."

We stand to leave. I tell her I'm not hungry. Then I insist on paying with some of Frank Montu's cookie-jar money.

I take one last look at the dining area and all the forest creatures, try to take one last mental picture that will allow me to remember anybody sitting here if I see them later. A couple dudes wearing a thug-style kind of look. Both are muscled up, but neither are eating.

Nobody goes to a buffet to talk and look around—not at sixty bucks a person—except for me.

Twenty-one

It takes approximately four different store visits within the Forum Shops Mall at Caesars before Pigtails finds a couple of things to try on. This gives me a few minutes to check text messages while she's in the dressing room. This does not feel like me—clandestine messaging with sex providers, not me at all.

Regarding sex providers, I don't judge. I know what they do: they uplift, entertain, provide physical affection as distraction, and most are healers by nature. The sneaking part is not me anymore. Sadly, I know I will flop at forgiving myself the way Jeanie suggested, which means I am in a lot of trouble if Ereshkigal meets me where I'm at, as Jeanie warned.

The first provider had answered back with a link for me to go to where I can prove my age by entering a credit card number. This is the one who texted back almost immediately during the Mr. Cowboy Boots restroom-stall scene—some auto-responding AI app of sorts.

No way, José.

The second provider wants me to take a pic of my driver's license held up next to my face and send it to her, which will prove I am real, or provide the name and number of a local provider who can vouch for my experience as a true "hobbyist," which I think means John, and not a scammer or law enforcement. She says her name is Bambi.

Hmmm. Interesting.

What intrigues me about Bambi is her response; it's well-written and concise, even though she's asking for a lot. This makes me feel like she likes what she does and that she's good at it.

What I am looking for is intricate and involves some cosplay.

I will hold off on deciding anything until I hear from the other two providers. I know time is not on my side. If I don't hear from the remaining two providers within the next hour, Bambi will be our winner.

I put the phone away and look up.

Pigtails is right there. She has a green dress thingy draped over her arm and a look on her face like she just caught the cat with the canary in its mouth.

"This little phone isn't the fastest at surfing the Internet," I tell her. It's better to stay ahead of the news as opposed to waiting for her to bust my balls. I continue by adding a cheesy joke. "I can still get on and off OnlyFans with some reasonable grace and aplomb."

"I bet," she fires back. "You're James Bond with that shit."

I don't have a retort. I am too tranced out on the two male characters I see at the back of the store—this women's clothing store. I see Thing One and Thing Two: the two muscled-up dudes from the buffet. The only two who weren't gorging themselves because they were too goddamn busy eyeballing everybody else.

"Wait," Pigtails says, catching how my eyes are staring beyond and behind her. The clever girl holds up her phone and uses the reflection on the screen to view the rest of the store behind her.

"You see those two earlier, maybe twenty minutes ago?" I ask, in a voice that's barely a mumble.

"Shit, Stevie Wonder would've seen them… they're so obvious," she whispers back. "They were eye-fucking every move I made at the buffet. First, I thought it was the no-bra-and-combat-boots look—you know I look hot. Now I see it's maybe something more."

"As soon as you find what you're going to buy here, let's fly."

"I already found it," she answers, and holds up the dress in her hand.

Pigtails pays for the dress and two other things. We leave through the opposite side of Caesars we came in through. Then we walk in the opposite direction of where we're parked.

Outside, we grab a cab. I tell the driver to take us to the Outlets.

Pigtails gives me a questioning look.

"The Outlets are famous for having the best prices on the best of what's trending. One green dress for Scotland is hardly going to do you," I tell her. "Besides, Frank Montu wants me to run up two of his credit cards—run 'em close to maxed, then get a credit increase. Loading you up with some outfits will do it."

"Yeah?" Pigtails fires back. "Sometimes you say things—the way it comes out, man—you sound like you are Frank Montu."

As soon as the cab starts moving, both Pigtails and I turn in our seats and watch out the rear window. I can feel the cab driver's eyes burning into our backs with a WTF kind of curiosity.

Twenty-two

On our way to the Outlets, we have our driver stop at four of the smaller sportsbooks we'd hit the day before. Picking up Pigtails' winnings is, thus far, smooth. I am able to sneak in another bathroom break where I triage my text messages from the remaining sex providers.

The third provider to answer back informs me that she is only doing incalls these days. Her ad is in error. No more outcalls. Ever. I cross her off my list.

So far, Bambi is in the lead. One more provider left to hear from, and if they don't work, I will hire Bambi or scan for more providers to choose from. Due to time constraints, Bambi is likely going to be the choice.

The big thing I like about the Outlets is that the place is shaped like a classic American mall from the Big Hair 1980s. There is something about the vibe and the look that reminds me of *Free Fallin'* by Tom Petty—three stories, a long fairway running down the middle, stores crammed together and lining each side of the fairway. Teenagers in love all over the place.

Pigtails immediately likes how there are food courts at each end of the mall. We are there barely five minutes, and she's got herself a Cinnabon lathered in cream cheese frosting and butter. The girl is skinny as a weed, and she eats like this all day. I try to forget that we were at the granddaddy buffet of all buffets just an hour ago.

What I love best about the mall floor plan are the glass bridges that cross from one side to the other, always above the escalators. Pigtails and I cross many, many times, looping back again and again. The bridges are makeshift observation posts.

Any followers?

None that we can see. But I can feel the followers trolling the Vegas waters for our scents. The way I feel them reminds me of growing up in Santa Cruz in the 1970s. Everybody surfed, and when you surfed, you knew there were great white sharks close, lurking. You couldn't see them, but you could feel them close and ready to eat you.

I can't tell if Pigtails can feel the Eightball sharks. I know she's nervous, and I can see she's getting jumpy. My suspicion is that she's waiting for that text to come in letting her know the passport is ready. Her mind is all about that text, and she will be distracted until that text happens. She's also wound up knowing all her cash and prepaid cards are in the olive-drab USMC MOLLE pack hanging off my back—she won't say she's uncomfortable about it, but I can tell. I wouldn't entirely trust me either.

She knows that during these last few days and these next couple of hours, she's the daughter I never had; treating her like my daughter is a vehicle through which I get a chance to vent out the best love I can muster and see what that looks like. I always knew the love I had to give was barely a puff of warm gruel. Now we'll see, and we'll know what's what—what Ereshkigal wants me to see: the true face I have for so long hidden from my sight and deprecated when I could.

Three clothing purchases later and, outside the mall, we grab another cab. We pay the driver to give us a couple of laps around the mall to see if anybody's following. Then we direct our driver to the remaining sportsbooks to collect Pigtails' winnings.

We just finish our second of the last four sportsbook stops when the driver makes two lane changes, does a big loop, and then changes lanes again while speeding up.

"What are you doing?" Pigtails asks.

"Hush," the driver answers.

"What are we doing, brother?" I ask.

"You two. I thought you were missing some gears, but now I see. You are right."

"Right about what?" I ask. I know the answer and turn in my seat so I can see out the back window. What I can see in the mirrors isn't enough. Pigtails turns with me—a slow and smooth turn.

"Yeah. You see?" the driver barks. "A modest sedan, clearly a rent-a-car. The kind you get at the airport. We make too many turns and they're still back there. We do a big circle; they do the same circle."

"How?" Pigtails growls.

I don't know how. Some kind of tracker on her person or in the cash, and she just didn't catch it. But all the cash has been laundered, and no tracker was ever found. And we are so close. Two sportsbooks left to stop at and collect her winnings—I was so hoping to complete this unscathed.

A loud cellphone ringtone sets off. Pigtails scrambles and pulls out her phone. She looks at her phone and then yelps with glee.

"It's ready. It's ready... man... it rains, it pours."

The passport.

I tell the driver to see if he can shake our follower. Pigtails tells him there's a $200 tip if he can.

"Where is your final, final destination?" the driver asks.

"Old School!" Pigtails barks at me, ignoring the driver. "Let's get the passport, I get to the airport, like you said, and that's that."

"Airport? Which airport?" the driver yells. "One is big, one is small. Lots of security at both.

Maybe I do not need to lose your follower—too much security for them at the airport..."

"Hold on there, sassafras," I coo to Pigtails. The cab of the car is filling up; I can feel the crackle of electricity. "We skip steps and rush, mistakes will be made. We stick to the plan. We grab that passport, pick up the last of your winnings, FedEx your cards, then we go straight to the airport—"

"Where is your stop going to be?" the driver asks loudly. "I lose these guys, easy for me. Where am I taking you after that?"

I tell the driver where we're headed to pick up the passport: the USPS location. I make eye contact with him in the rearview mirror. He can clearly see the question in my face.

"Okay, okay," the driver yells. "I will help you. I will lose our tail. Then we go to USPS. The reason I ask: I will make it double safe for you. I will lose your followers, then I make it double safe for you. You go to USPS with zero worries."

I doubt the zero-worries part. "Do it," I tell him.

The driver speeds up a bit—not sudden or exaggerated. He drives onto an expressway, wedges himself between two trucks, then slips off the expressway.

Both Pigtails and I watch through the rear window.

The follower misses the exit we take.

"You did it, captain," I tell the driver. I dig around for Frank Montu's wallet with the cookie-jar money in it. Bobby Dynamite's money is long gone.

"I have not!" the driver whispers. "I appreciate your faith. You saw one follower, and I saw two. An SUV and a sedan. The sedan missed out, and the SUV is on us. The SUV communicates with the sedan; they will both be back."

Fuck me.

"You're right," Pigtails adds, watching out the rear window. "I see that SUV, and it was there twenty turns ago."

"Take it easy, take it easy," the driver tells us. "I do too much, they know we know. I stay cool, we can slip them. Get ready to get out when we stop; do exactly as I say."

I look over at Pigtails. We both give each other the wide-eyed WTF look.

Back to the front, I watch the driver change lanes, make a turn, then another turn. He pulls a key card with a clip hanging from it out of his shirt breast pocket, all the while watching the mirrors, the road in front of us, and never once driving erratically.

The driver reaches backward, handing me the key card. "Take it," he snaps. "I am going to drive through the 'employee only' loading area of a building called the 'Signature.' This place is part of MGM—basically timeshare units converted into apartments. I work there, and I drive as a side gig, too. You go in the entrance. As soon as you are inside, walk straight back. Big elevator right there.

Get on the elevator. Hit the button labeled L7. Got that? L7."

"L7," I bark back. I can feel Pigtails staring at me, shocked and confused.

"L7 takes you to the tram that runs from the Signature basement to the crazy huge parking garage at Harrah's. Two tracks going back and forth. If you have to wait at all, three minutes at the most. I drop you at the Signature, I lose your friends, then I meet you at the bottom floor of Harrah's parking garage. Only residents that live and work at the Signature know about the tram and can use the tram. You need the key card I gave you."

Pigtails' wild look burning into the side of my head intensifies.

I answer with no look at all. I'm trying to think.

Our driver makes two left turns, and now we are running on a frontage road to the Miracle Mile and Planet Hollywood. Then he makes a quick right and slows to a stop in front of a narrow walk and unmarked double doors.

"Go now, friends. Bottom floor of Harrah's parking garage. I will come in with no followers."

I open the door and climb out, shouldering the MOLLE pack.

Pigtails climbs out and bolts down the narrow path toward the unmarked double doors.

I trot after her.

Our driver didn't ask for his payment

before we ran off. On the surface, this looks like it authenticates his sincerity; he really plans on being at Harrah's. The hardened part of me, the ex-con part of me, is of a completely different mind.

When the newly convicted first get to the pen, lots of strangers try to give advice, hear your story, be generous. And if you want to survive, you have to say no. You have to bond with your ethnicity group, keep your eyes off anybody else, and accept no favors.

There are no favors—any goodness you accept, you'll be expected to pay it back.

Or worse.

In a place like Pelican Bay, when you get there, you are going to be put into one of two categories: have a wife or be a wife.

This dude helping us out, and then not wanting the ride fare—I'm suspicious. He's going to monetize the fact that he knows exactly where we're headed, and he will leverage that knowledge with the two vehicles on our ass. This is my thinking.

I finally catch up to Pigtails at the elevator. She's got the L7 button pressed. The doors close, and we start going down.

I am obviously behind the power curve, washed up, because homegirl Pigtails, as soon as the elevator doors close, says to me, "Buddy set us up, didn't he? Directions he gave us go nowhere, some dead end. He'll flag down our followers and sell what he knows."

"I don't know, kitten," I mumble back. "You don't know either; otherwise, we wouldn't be in this elevator."

I marvel at how quick she is, so smart. I wish I knew more—knew anything—about her parents. I would tell them outright what a doll they brought into the world, what an amazing being their daughter is.

"I ain't going to Harrah's," she growls. "Fuck no. First chance we get, grab an Uber and get back to your buddy Frank Monkey's car."

Montu. Frank Montu, I want to tell her, but the me that I was seems so long ago.

Twenty-three

The elevator stops at L7. The doors open. We both step out, stand there stupidly, looking left and right and then left again, like two cats watching a ball fire back and forth in a tennis match.

The hallway running to the right ends with stairs going up, and a big sign tells you exactly that: STAIRS.

The hallway to the left, which is long and dimly lit, opens up about 150 feet ahead, but I can't tell if that's a tram stop of any kind. Halfway down the hallway on the left, there's an alcove with at least one vending machine and an ATM visible. There's probably more in the alcove than I can see.

The elevator behind us makes a noise, the doors shut, and it starts going back up. Both Pigtails and I jump at the sound. What really startles us is the idea that someone from above just called the elevator.

We turn and begin a light jog down the long hallway on the left, with the alcove positioned at the halfway mark of its length. We jog past the alcove—two vending machines, two chairs bolted to the floor, and an ATM. Some kind of makeshift break area.

I keep looking back, and so does Pigtails. We're both waiting for whoever it was who called the elevator, expecting them to show up any minute.

We reach the end of the long hallway. To the right, there's a long bench. A big sign above the bench reads: HARRAH'S / PARKING.

Pigtails takes a seat on the bench and hugs her knees like she's cold. Her mind is rifling through files, looking for an answer to a problem, and I'm pretty sure I know what the problem is.

I unshoulder the pack and set it at her feet.

"You know what's wrong. I don't need to tell you," Pigtails says. "Homeboy driver sold what he knows about us to some big tippers—so he hopes. Thinks he's going to have a quick talk with the followers. Easy to get wound up with ideas about two carloads' worth of people tipping him and rewarding him for sending us into a corner."

"Maybe. Maybe not," I answer back. A part of me believes she's right. I lightly kick the bag with my foot. "I'm going back down the hall. There's a shadow spot next to those vending machines. You text me when the tram comes. If I don't show or text back, that means our buddy burned us and I'm tangled with the company that came after us. Get on the tram, but don't get off at Harrah's.

Somewhere else. Anywhere else. Call an Uber, taxi—whatever—go straight to that USPS and get your passport. Go to a FedEx place and ship your prepaids, then straight to the airport. One, two, three."

"You really think that driver burned us?" she asks. She's looking up at me with hopeful eyes. Sad eyes. Eyes like she knows the answer and wants me to negate the nightmare answer she already knows is real.

"I think he figured out if he could guide us into a spot where we're cornered, the two carloads of people chasing us would be real generous to him —a bigger dollar than what he was going to get from us." I pause and dig out Frank Montu's keys and toss them to Pigtails. "Use these," I add. "You don't want to do Uber, I wouldn't blame you. I know Frank Montu, and he would insist you take these keys and his car."

"That double-crossing fuckface driver will lose his keycard," she adds.

"No, he won't. Look at it. Not even his picture on it, I bet. He found it, or somebody left it in his car. We didn't even need the keycard to get down here. Did you notice that? Part of his ruse to earn our trust. He got a little creative when it was time to improvise."

Pigtails looks at the keycard and then back up at me.

"It scares me that you knew that."

I don't answer. I wave my phone at her to

pantomime texting me, and then I jog back down the hallway with the alcove.

There's so much electricity in the air again —static electricity.

This will be my big moment. Trouble is coming, and I'll find out if I can handle what Ereshkigal thought I might handle.

I glance ahead at the elevator before ducking into the alcove.

The doors slide open, but no one steps out.

They're in there. Wanna bet?

Inside the vending machine alcove, I skirt behind one of the machines just as the elevator chimes, signaling the doors are closing. Whoever was inside is out now... on their way to me.

The vending machine's hum is too loud, so I shift to a narrow gap between the ATM and the other machine.

I still can't hear enough—or at least it feels that way. But I can see the reflections of the overhead lights on the hallway floor. If whoever's pursuing us moves slowly enough, I'll spot their approach in the reflection. And with any luck, I'll have just enough time to step out and intercept them.

That's all I need to do: get in their way, give Pigtails an edge of time.

Christ, I can feel the pulsing pressure of pent-up static electricity getting bigger, but the air is still. Then the tune of *The Bridge on the River Kwai*. Just whistling away—the same whistler from before.

Mr. Cowboy Boots.

I'm excited. Here comes my trouble. The whistle, the sound of his boot heels hitting the concrete floor.

What's he look like? Is he the Boss of Gum fella from earlier?

I know what that tall and gangly bastard looks like.

Has the mystery and unknown factor of danger I might pose wore off?

Pigtails knew it would. She'd called it earlier —soon as we have the money laundered and sportsbook cash retrieved, our friends will pounce.

We are so close to having everything laundered and Pigtails getting away.

Now, how in the hell do they keep finding us? This part is the big mystery to me.

I hear the heels stop. Then the whistling stops, just out of view from the nook in which I have myself tucked away.

He knows where I'm at?

This isn't fair. How's he know where I'm at?

In a warped way, I'm relieved. If he's focused on me, he's not focused on Pigtails.

As if on cue, my flip phone vibrates. I take a quick peek.

PIGTAILS:
Tram is here!!! Get
out here, Punchy!

Not a chance. She's serious as hell, too,

because she's calling me by the Punchy moniker.

So sorry, girl. No time to answer—can't afford to keep my eyes off the hallway for more than a second; you-know-who is about to show himself. I know he's here to grab her and her money, and I'm here to make sure he gets nowhere.

He will get nowhere.

Lord, it hurts not to text her back. I always felt special when she called me Old School. In my mind, I'm trying to will her to remember what I said and take heed of what I said. I told her: *You text me when the tram comes. If I don't show or text back, that means our buddy really burned us, and I'm tangled with the company that came after us. Get on the tram, but don't get off at Harrah's. Somewhere else. Anywhere else. Call an Uber, taxi—whatever. Go straight to that USPS and get your passport. Go to a FedEx place and ship your prepaids, then straight to the airport. One, two, three.*

Twenty-four

"You want to step out so I can see you, sweetie?" Mr. Cowboy Boots tells me.

I recognize his voice just fine.

The chewing-gum shithead. Boss of Gum.

I'm too slow to answer.

"Or you want me to step in so you can see me?" he continues. "I step in... you'll be cornered. That little hidey spot was a good idea, assuming you could surprise me. No surprise for me. I can smell you. You stink like some kind of... ethnic."

Ethnic? What kind of disturbo, bigoted comment is that?

I don't say anything. All my life I have been a counterpuncher, even before I found myself stuck in Bobby Dynamite's body. Let the other guy react to my stillness.

Make Cowboy Boots be the one to initiate— that's the best recipe.

"One..." Mr. Cowboy Boots coos at me.

I see. What a drama queen. He's giving me a countdown now. This guy has seen too many cheesy 1980s thriller movies.

Here's the deal: at Pelican Bay, I never boxed, but I did fight for my life. I learned to kick, bite, and eye-gouge. I also learned to never start the fight—leave that bad karma for the other guy—but always hit first.

Hit first with everything you have. Don't wait for the count of three. Hit as soon as the aggressor gets to the count of two.

A brief pause from Mr. Cowboy Boots, and then he says, "Two…"

I step out from the nook, duck, and run forward into the nearest and only figure I see. I ram my head into his groin, grab his left leg with my right arm and his right leg with my left arm. I push forward with all my leg strength and gradually lift up. Then I slow my forward momentum and let gravity pull him down. I'm like a dock worker with a long sack of potatoes over his shoulder who rushes forward and then slows himself so the sudden drop in momentum and gravity pulls the potatoes onto the ground.

Lucky for me, he is lean, tall, and wearing jeans—he falls like a stiff and creaky old tree. We hit that polished concrete floor with a deep thud, me on top and him on his back. He immediately brings his knees up so I can't mount him and begins battering my temples and face with his fists, and he is not throwing pillow punches.

I'm not going to mount him. Not even try.

Instead, I ram my head forward. I use

every bit of momentum I can muster to slam my forehead into his chin.

The impact is dense and crisp. I feel like I whacked my forehead against the ball of a towing hitch. I am seeing stars—I hit his chin so hard.

I still will not try to mount him.

I decide to bite into his face. I fit his entire nose and part of a cheek into my mouth and bite down as hard as I can. He is not ready for this type of attack.

I bite and scream my best war cry.

I can feel his body stiffen beneath me. He isn't stiffening from pain—too much adrenaline. He won't feel the pain yet.

He stiffens from surprise and fear.

He wasn't ready for the headshot to the groin, grabbing his legs, and being dumped onto his back. The headbutt to the chin, also a surprise. He isn't anywhere close to imagining I would chew into his face like a rabid zombie, and here I am.

I pull my mouth away for just a brief second and then bite again with a bigger purchase. It's funny. In that brief gap between bites, when I pull back for just a second, I glimpse one of Bobby Dynamite's teeth stuck in the dude's cheek.

This second bite is better because it covers more surface area—I grab more meat, cheek, and eyelid—and I am really venting out some scary animal-zombie attacking sounds, my war cry cranked up.

I didn't feel the first tooth come out, but

during this second bite, I do feel another two teeth come out.

I don't care. This is for Pigtails. I let this guy get too close as it is.

Pop!

Wild. What sounds like a firecracker going off beneath a pillow causes both of us to flinch and freeze up. Then I remember I don't have anything that makes that kind of noise, which means he does.

So, I scramble.

I scramble for the arm of his that isn't striking at me, scratching and clawing at my face. Shit, that arm of his that isn't busy hitting me has something in it that made a pop!

I am a bad scrambler. There's a hot pain in my side, like a red-hot screwdriver has been stabbed into me.

Okay. I guess I've been shot.

Run, Pigtails! I scream in my mind. *Get gone! USPS, FedEx, airport… one, two, three.*

I keep trying to grab and wrestle the arm that I am sure, judging by the fire in my side, has a gun in it. The way the pain in my side is stabbing upward and at an angle of hot fire, I just don't move well.

The sonofabitch got me good. He really got me.

Run, Pigtails!
I am so sorry. I flopped again—run!

Something dark and made of leather cracks

me on the side of the head—a glancing blow, not a direct hit. Mr. Cowboy Boots, however, does get directly hit by the dark and leathery heavy object. I hear the thud and feel the reverberations loud and clear.

Mr. Cowboy Boots thrusts his hips upward enough that I am tossed off him now.

I wiggle and writhe as quickly as I can to my knees, and there is Pigtails, pounding Mr. Gum Cowboy Boots in the head again and again with one of her combat boots.

Christ, look at her swing that boot like a hammer!

I marvel at how she uses the same gusto that must've been used when the last Irishman pounded the last tie into the Union Pacific Railroad.

My blue-haired buddy disobeyed what I'd said earlier and instead came to my rescue.

I reach for Mr. Cowboy Boots' right arm and grab the small piece with which he shot me. It pulls away easily—he has no grip strength.

I can see he's out cold.

"Okay, okay," I tell Pigtails. "We're good. Ease up, girl."

She doesn't ease up a damn thing. She never listens to me.

I reach a free hand up to signal her to stop. My hand is dripping in blood.

The blood stops her.

Pigtails drops the boot and kneels right

there at my side.

"I'm alright," I tell her.

I position the small handgun for use, just in case dumbass wakes from his combat-boot-forced nap.

Sheesh, this popper he nailed me with is small—the size of a pack of cigarettes. .22 caliber. It doesn't even feel like metal. I'm thinking Mr. Cowboy Boots popped me with one of those 3D-printed guns called a "stinger." Shit, I was in the can, and all the dudes with armed robbery rap sheets wanted a stinger. You can hide one anywhere.

"We need to move, Old School. Won't be long before somebody comes down this hall. You were screaming sounds from a horror movie. And I am damn sure you need an emergency room."

"I need one thing from homie before we get out of here," I tell her.

"What could you possibly want from this trash?"

"How they kept tracking us down, and if he's working for Eightball or Eightball's dad. Eightball strikes me as someone smart as a bowling ball. Why is a psychopath, clearly very intelligent and intuitive, working for a moron king?"

"Those are stupid questions. How you gonna get him to answer?"

"Watch." Then I start slapping the wounds on Mr. Cowboy Boots' face. I slap hard.

His eyes start to move.

"I have your stinger," I tell him. "This is a little two-shot. You sunk one into me. You refuse to answer my next question, I'll sink this second round into Winky." I firmly smash the barrel of the stinger into Mr. Cowboy Boots' groin. "Like that," I add.

Pigtails issues the briefest of giggles.

Mr. Cowboy Boots doesn't say anything, but with the one good eye that didn't get torn up when I chewed his face, he gives me a steady and consistent stare. The darkest stare I have ever seen. Makes me understand I will have to put this man down, or he will simply keep trying and trying to get at me and Pigtails... until he does.

"What have you been using? And be specific," I tell him.

"What have I been using for what, peabrain?" he replies as best he can. Some of his lip was chewed off with portions of his nose and cheek, making it real tough to put together a sentence.

"You've been very consistent at keeping with us. Haven't missed a beat. I know how, but I want to hear you say it."

He doesn't answer. He just laughs.

With what strength I can muster, which isn't easy because I can feel blood draining down my side and soaking my left pant leg, I press the stinger as deeply into his groin as I can.

"You really want me to blow out your junk?"

"Your shoe," he mumbles. "The first afternoon, I stuck a guy in a car to watch that whore's Tiki Room apartment... I knew Zipper was a fuckup. Cover my ass is the name of my game. You showed up. You took your shoes off and left them outside the door. I sent a little Chink that works for me to glue a tracker into your heel. The little gook is good at that... goddamn cobbler when he isn't doing crime."

I look up at Pigtails. She nods, our silent understanding shared between us. If this man lives, he'll track the two of us until he gets us. I nod my head for her to turn away. As soon as she does, I lift the stinger from Mr. Cowboy Boots' groin and reposition the barrel onto his sternum.

I don't wait for him to flinch.

Pop!

Neither of us checks to see if he's dead. We don't need to.

I kick off my shoes.

"Help me get his boots off of him and onto my feet," I tell her.

She helps me get both boots on. I hate watching her face be sad and in pain beneath the hoodie, her brow furrowed.

She's worried about me.

"It's not that bad," I tell her. "There's a little blood... always makes things look worse. I'm okay."

"You have a hole in your side, you asshole. Now what?" she nags at me.

"One, two, three... USPS to get your passport, FedEx, and then airport. One... two... three."

"You're out of your mind," she barks. She picks up one of my shoes, then the other, and examines the bottoms. "We wasted ten extra seconds on that psychopath. We'd have to be dumb as rocks not to believe we had a tracker of some kind stuck to us somewhere. He only told us what we were suspecting anyway."

"As soon as you walk through the TSA security gate, I'm going to urgent care. An hour from now, tops," I try to reassure her.

It's time for me to stand. She is helping. My side is burning so bad she has to do most of the work, and I am panting more than a phone sex performer with a mortgage.

"You son of a bitch," she tells me. "You drive me around, you talk to imaginary friends, and right when I start liking you because you are a genuine weirdo like me, you get shot protecting me... this is not the crappy ending I want. You happy now? The old guilt gone now that you did a good deed?"

Both of us hear the elevator get called again.

Pigtails gets her combat boot back on, shoulders the MOLLE pack, and we both walk huddled together toward the tram area.

Pigtails mumbles at me through gritted teeth as we hobble along, "When we get back on the street, first chance I get, I'm buying you a black hoodie. You are way too bloody, babe."

Twenty-five

We catch the tram going the other direction, away from Harrah's. The cowboy boots feel okay for the short term. Pigtails wipes down the stinger and tosses it in the trash. We leave my shoe with the tracker glued into it on the tram. I am having a hard time imagining how I didn't notice my shoe had a small hole carved into the sole, and a tracker filling the hole, for goddamn two days. We stay on the tram for two stops and climb off at a stop that advertises a four-story candy store and a CVS.

"How many CCTV cameras do you think they had in that hallway where we left Fuckface Gum?" Pigtails asks.

"I have no idea. No doubt there are some. I'm just glad you had your hoodie up."

"Yeah, but what about you?"

"As long as we get you past that TSA security gate, I'll be fine," I answer her. "I told you from the get-go, this is my last ride. I have zero to lose."

"Get me on the plane, your imaginary friend Ereshkigal shows up and makes everything good—is that how you see it?"

My answer to her is a wince of pain.

"Yeah," she says. "The adrenaline is wearing off. You've got that thing in your side, and your teeth… I don't know what to say about your teeth. Some are gone. They were stuck into his face, man."

Sitting down, my side kills me. Standing up and walking, there's no pain, but feeling blood run down my side and then down my legs scares me.

The other thing that scares me is my long-running dilemma that's only half-solved. If I really knew all the ways Eightball and the late Mr. Cowboy Boots tracked us, I wouldn't necessarily need a rock-solid diversion—I could mislead them by using their tracking method to my advantage.

I know some of how they tracked us, and we tossed that shoe accordingly. I know there's likely more—some method I'm not aware of with which they are still tracking us. So far, they've been spot-on, which means I need to connect with Bambi and make a deal for her help with my diversion plan. If not Bambi, then someone else. It's not a matter of if they find us again; it's a matter of when —another scene like what went down with Mr. Cowboy Boots is not a solution.

Once we reach street level—and this is not a street I want to be on; it's the Strip—Pigtails drags me into the CVS. I walk slowly and stay close to her in case I get wobbly. She buys two black hoodies, gauze, peroxide, and a jug of Gatorade.

Outside CVS, we are two characters in black hoodies.

We take a cab to Frank Montu's car at Caesars. We pay the cabbie to stay until we back out and leave the Strip—Pigtails gives him the two hundred bucks she would have given the other driver if he hadn't presumably sold us to the crew pursuing us.

We have a four-bump plan mapped out, and I have an extra bump I can't share with Pigtails.

First bump: drive somewhere quiet and nondescript with a bathroom and off the Strip, where we stop my bleeding and protect my wound.

Second bump: get to that USPS office and get Pigtails' passport.

Third bump: FedEx her prepaids to Glasgow —and she still needs to pick a hotel there to send them to.

And the fourth bump: drive Pigtails to the airport.

This is no easy agenda we mapped out because she needs to reserve a flight along the way, and we need to hit the remaining two sportsbooks —that's at least thirty-six grand right there.

Additionally, somewhere between now and getting the passport, I need to text Bambi and cross my fingers she's available. When I play our agenda in my mind, all of this feels clear as mud.

At Frank Montu's car, Pigtails insists on

driving. We drive to the first Motel 8 we can find away from the Strip. Pigtails rents a room. We grab the Gatorade, gauze, peroxide, the MOLLE pack, and head inside.

Pigtails tries to bring the Jameson, and I tell her to leave it. Believe me, I would love a nip or two from that bottle. I can feel myself losing cabin pressure, and I have too many chores between this moment and my goal of getting Pigtails away to risk any of that with alcohol sloppiness.

In the bathroom, I strip down as best I can. Pigtails has to help me with my pants and my shirt. There is nothing pleasant about putting her through this process. I am embarrassed for this old and banged-up Bobby Dynamite body, and I am even more embarrassed I messed it up so quickly and so thoroughly.

"You're an asshole. Look at you," she rasps out. She's crying.

It kills me that she's crying like this because I know it hurts her to see me hurt. I haven't had anybody care since my Jeanie and Becky days. Pigtails' nose is running with snot, and I feel like the world's most productive scoundrel for making her cry.

"You and your sonofabitch self," she adds.

"Wipe the wounds with peroxide—be real liberal. Put gauze over the holes, wrap me with an Ace bandage. Just like that—"

"I know what to do. Don't be a dick," she screams. "There's only one hole… so it's inside you.

How do you like that? You happy now? You got whatever kind of slug it was inside you. You get to fall on your sword and be a martyr like you wanted."

I don't answer. I'm feeling dizzy and don't want her to hear me slowly shorting out.

She finishes cleaning, stopping the bleeding, and wrapping me. I ask her to bring me my bag. I'll have to wear my clothes from the first night she met me. The ones I had on today are ruined. She brings my clothes from the car. I ask her to leave me alone a few minutes here in the bathroom.

I text Bambi once I'm alone with the door shut. I let her know I am about to text over her requirements.

What I really want is just a chance to lie down and have a nap.

Pigtails knocks on the door. "You don't be passing out on me. I'll knock you out, Old School," she yells through the door.

"Give me five. Five, and I'll be good to go."

I take a few swigs of Gatorade. I take a camera pic of my driver's license, Bobby's suspended license, and text it to Bambi. Then I text a very specific list of what I want her to do. I include how much I will pay her as soon as she walks in the door, and how much she will receive as soon as her performance begins.

Talk about endings. Here I am in a Motel 8 bathroom. I am sitting on the toilet, drinking warm Gatorade and texting a prostitute a list of things I want her to do, how I want her to dress, and what kind of wig I want her to have on. I also have a bullet hole in my side, and the tiny copper hornet of a slug is somewhere inside me.

My God, what have I done with myself?

The icing on the crazy cake is knowing that four days ago I was a man named Frank Montu, and I shot myself in the head with the same Luger my old man used to put himself by.

Twenty-six

On the way to the USPS store, I make Pigtails stop at a grocery store. I buy a pound of liver and a box of Oreos. The liver is loaded with super vitamins in high doses. The Oreos are quick energy. I eat as best I can while she drives. The pain from my stinger wound comes in flurries—some so bad that all I can do is hug myself, close my eyes, and hold on.

Twice while she's driving, my phone vibrates, letting me know a text has come through.

Bambi is my guess.

"Who's texting, Old School?"

I glance at the phone, just to make sure it's Bambi.

"My diversion plan. I'll tell you all about it once we get that passport, book your flight, and pick up your last two sports bets. Then I'll spill the beans."

"Just say it. You don't need to stall. When you stall, you're not only an asshole—you're a double-stuffed asshole."

At the USPS place, I insist we park in the handicapped spot. For the first time ever, she agrees with something I say.

"I'll wait in the car with the motor running while you run in," I tell her.

We both look around nervously, and then she runs in.

I read Bambi's message.

Bambi's on board with everything, with one condition: we do the performance at a hotel she trusts. She gives me the names of two to choose from. I pick one and text her that I'll be in place in an hour. Bambi answers back that she needs two hours. I text her back: *Fine.*

As soon as I fire off that last text, Pigtails comes barreling out of the USPS office. I've never seen a girl so happy. Happy is what I need. I need all the happy I can summon for when I tell Pigtails about my sex-worker friend, Bambi—my young pigtailed revolutionary is going to blow her stack and knock my block off.

We pull away from the USPS office, and my worry genes start busting my balls again. The Frank Montu body. Surely someone found it by now. One more thing to worry about is getting pulled over. APB? I don't know. I have a gunshot wound and Bobby's suspended license—talking to any kind of LE will go over like a lead balloon.

Twenty-seven

The second-to-last sportsbook is easy-breezy, lemon squeezy.

"In and out. No problem. No followers," Pigtails tells me, climbing back into the car. "But you look rough, bro. This hurts watching you... I love you, but you look fish-belly pale."

My side with the bullet hole is on fire. I know it's my imagination this early in the game, but I feel like poison is flowing out from the copper hornet buried in my innards. I can taste and smell metal.

What Pigtails just said doesn't help. I know she's right.

The last sportsbook stop on our chore list is a horrid mess. Cars, people, buses. Thankfully, they have a well-manned and talented valet crew. My only mistake was thinking I could go inside with her. I have no idea how I walked as far as I did.

Back outside and loading into Montu's car, I convince Pigtails to let me drive. She knows I'm in pain and refuses.

"You should see yourself walk. I can't imagine you driving. If you weren't bundled in a black hoodie, you'd be handcuffed to a hospital gurney right now, and I'd be in jail. You're bleeding, and you walk like a crackhead. Your face is pale, and your cheeks are sucked up, man. This is killing me, watching you go down in flames to help me."

"You have the sharper eye," I tell her. "I need you to watch for followers, and I'll do the driving part. Right before that fuckface Uber driver burned us, there was a sedan and an SUV. I only spotted the sedan; you spotted both. You have the keener eye, girl."

In my mind, I'm thinking if we have zero followers while going to FedEx, there's no reason for my diversion—I text Bambi that it's off, and we go straight to the airport. If followers show up, however—and it sure feels like they're watching us now—then we need to launch my diversion by going straight to the hotel I told Bambi we'd meet her at.

We travel three turns, and we are on a freeway. Pigtails tells me, "Bro, turn off the freeway and then get back on again. Go a little way, one or two exits, and then rinse and repeat."

"Why? You see something?" I ask. The words sound horrible. I need to stand soon. Sitting like this is really painful, as painful as walking was.

"It's worse, and you know it," Pigtails tells me.

"Only if I sit for too long. I get up and stand a bit, the pain flattens out."

"I'm talking about our posse of followers, bro, not your bullet hole. I don't need updates on your bullet hole—bandaged or not, I know you're bleeding out. We got three followers so far. Just drive like I said."

"Three? Fuck me."

I rinse and repeat.

Pigtails doesn't need to tell me the answer. I know they're there.

"Then we use my diversion," I tell her.

"The secret diversion you haven't shared with me since I started asking three days ago?" she asks, her head swiveling from mirror to mirror and sometimes just flat-out staring out the rear window.

"I'm going to tell you a hotel name. You look it up and give me directions."

She doesn't answer. I watch her nod through my peripheral vision. The nod is barely perceptible.

I tell her the hotel name.

Pigtails looks up the hotel on her flip phone. "Man, you like the bottom-of-the-barrel kind of places, don't you?" she tells me. "You're not going to shake them—they stay on us somehow no matter what. They'll follow us right into the hotel parking lot. We somehow manage to scoot inside, and they'll stay right there until we come out."

"And that is exactly how I want to run it."

"What about FedEx and shipping of the prepaids?"

"You'll have to do that after I divert our friends. On your way to the airport, throw them in your luggage. I bet there's a FedEx kiosk in several places at the airport."

"You're not going to take me to the airport?" she asks. I can hear sadness and alarm in her voice.

"I am going to be entertaining the followers. I will keep them deeply engaged."

"Engaged enough I don't have to knock anyone out with my combat boot?"

"Let's hope not. That hallway scene was not planned out. I am very grateful. You saved my ass, and I know it. This diversion we're talking about right now is planned out."

"All three follower cars look full," she adds. "So at least a half-dozen adoring fans are on us, bro."

I don't answer that one. I sneak a few quick peeks at her face and the looks she is trying to hide.

Shame and fear.

She wants to worry, and she wants to feel like this is her fault. She's prepping to hate herself when something bad happens to me.

Someone along the way taught her about self-loathing. Someone before Zipper.

Twenty-eight

T he knocking beat of the "Shave and a Haircut... Two Bits" rhythm resounds from our hotel room door.

Pigtails freezes in place.

I pantomime for her to hold tight. I do my best to gesture for calm. "This is part of my diversion, bro," I coo. "Have a seat. I am going to answer the door, let in our friend, and explain everything." Pigtails already knows all this; I am only saying it to make myself feel better.

I double-check through the gap in the drapes to make sure our followers are still out there in the parking lot, reassuring myself they're not trying to come in now. Our adoring groupies are still outside, smoking and sitting in their respective vehicles. I know it won't be long before they storm the gates, and what I am about to act out, I want and need them to see every bit of it.

"Let in our friend?" Pigtails asks with disdain. "That's *your* friend. I don't want to sit. How about *you* sit?"

"Please," I plead. "This is important. Can we groove along? We need this. I will introduce you as June. Not Pigtails. It's not that I don't trust this woman I'm about to let in, but I don't trust her."

Pigtails sits. She tells me under her breath, "We wired off a ton of cash. The prepaid cards are going to be FedExed out on my ride to Harry Reid. All I have is the remainder of the winnings from the sportsbook bets. You roll me now, I lose about forty grand, and it's my own dumb fault for not seeing the Jekyll-and-Hyde side of you. No matter the man, men are flippy-floppy."

I don't answer. I know she's venting her nervousness, her anger at Zipper and every deadbeat before him. She's also venting the pain of goodbyes. An hour from now—maybe two—she'll be at the airport and through the security gates. Never see each other again. I know it's only been three and a half days together, but I am not ready to say goodbye either.

The upcoming goodbye is starting early with the big hurt.

I slink over to the door and give the peephole a thorough glance. There's Bambi, holding up a peace sign with her right hand, just as I had requested earlier. She's dressed brightly in a Little Red Riding Hood outfit, just as I had requested.

I can see blonde tresses peeking out from beneath the hood. It would be safe to bet she did one other thing I had requested earlier as well:

danced and pranced and made a big scene coming into the hotel. Made a scene reserving a room here at the hotel. Anyone in the parking lot would have seen her dance and enter. All of our followers out there, waiting with bated breath for Pigtails, would have seen Bambi's show.

"Hello," I whisper, swinging the door open and waving her in.

"You Old School?" she asks. Then she walks right in before I can answer, squeezing my bicep before stopping right beside me.

"I am." I shut the door and hand her an envelope with all that remains of Frank Montu's cash—he won't be using it. I tell Bambi, "Here's the first half of what we agreed on. You'll get the second half once we go over the plan and you change outfits."

"Brother, you should have seen my dancing and prancing entrance. Anybody that has a pulse out there in that parking lot got revved up— and the corpses, too." Bambi makes the briefest of glances into the envelope. "You paid extra, sugar. Thank you, thank you," she adds.

I am amazed at how fast she counts the cash —counts with just a glance.

Using my hands and my best smile for direction, I guide Bambi to the center of the room. I can see Pigtails watching us. Bambi does a slight twirl with a flourish. The Red Riding Hood skirt portion of the outfit is a mini-mini skirt. I can't imagine Pigtails not liking that, given her penchant for mini-mini shorts.

"June," I say to Pigtails, "this is Bambi. Bambi, this is June." Then, after a pause, I add, "Have a seat, Bambi. Anywhere you'll be comfortable."

Bambi sits in a reading chair across from Pigtails.

"This'll be good," Pigtails mumbles. "I can't wait to see what's about to play out."

"Bambi, would you like some coffee or Jameson? I'm afraid that's all we have. And water, of course."

"I'm okay for now," she answers. "I agree with lovely June. Let's hear the plan one more time. That'll melt the ice in the air. I remember everything we discussed via text, but saying it now with all players present is medicine."

I sit and look at Pigtails as I explain things. I went over the plan so many times texting with Bambi that I imagine Bambi sees me as someone as stable as a dog in a cat factory... with some heavy OCD.

"Bambi is going to undress," I tell Pigtails. "Completely. You, June, are going to undress completely. Bambi will dress in your clothes, June, and you will dress in Bambi's."

I can see Pigtails start to protest. I know what she's going to bring up.

"Bambi," I chortle, "show June the two sets of hair you brought."

Bambi pulls down the hood of her Red

Riding Hood outfit. She's wearing a porn-star blonde wig. She pulls it off and hands it to Pigtails. Then she reaches into her bag and brings out a bright blue wig, combed and styled into pigtails.

"You can help me put this on, adjust it so it's as pretty as your hair," Bambi tells Pigtails.

"This is your plan? A stunt double... a pole-dancer stunt double?" Pigtails snarls at me from across the small room.

"Just hear me out," I snap. I try to say it firmly. I know what Pigtails is doing. She's looking to argue, to delay, to add some intensity to these last moments. She's not ready for the show to end.

Neither am I.

We have to do this.

She's going to the goddamn airport, and that's that.

"After you two switch outfits, Bambi will give you the key card to the room she reserved here. And you will give her one thousand dollars cash to cover the room and her time with me today. Bambi and I, looking exactly like you and me, will leave here—clandestine, really playing up how you move and groove. Once we're gone, and you see those followers out there chase after Bambi and me, you will take all your things and go down to the room Bambi reserved. You will go into the room, lock the door, stay away from windows, until I text you."

"When you text me? Text me what?" Pigtails asks.

"When I text you, you call for a limo. Have the limo text or call when they get here so you don't wait around outside. In fact, don't leave the room until that limo is here and they're screaming for you. You go outside, hood up, sunglasses, hair hidden—full Red Riding Hood get-up."

"Okay," Pigtails tells me. "I leave this room to go to Little Red Riding Hood's room, dressed in that Halloween costume. Lock myself down until I hear from you. Call a limo. Easy. Where are you at? And another thing—over two days we've been running with the MOLLE pack mostly on your back—how do you want to handle that?"

"As soon as you two switch outfits, you empty out that MOLLE pack. I'll stuff it with a Bible and a couple of towels, make it look full, and Bambi's going to carry that when she and I leave—Bambi carrying the MOLLE pack and looking like you. Ten minutes from now, tops."

"Is that so?" Pigtails mutters. She gets up from her seat, scoots over to the window, and moves one side of the drapes ever so slightly, creating the tiniest of gaps. She peeks out the gap as she tells Bambi and me, "You tell Bambi who's out there yet?"

"He filled me in enough," Bambi blurts out. "I've been an entertainer for twelve years. There ain't no kind of angry spouse, psycho character, stalker, power-tripper meltdown I haven't seen."

"Gum was no joke. Eightball is no joke," chimes Pigtails.

"The tougher the name, the harder they fall is how I know things go," Bambi fires back. Then, staring right at me, Bambi says, "Can I tell her the other part?"

"Tell it," Pigtails and I both blurt out in unison.

The fact that we are so well harmonized saddens me even more—adding to the heaviness. I'll be leading the followers away, and no more Old School and Pigtails show.

Bambi says, "I don't care who you have following me and Old School when we blow this place, as long as I get paid. You've already paid me half, and I am quite confident I will be paid the other half as promised. Following me back to my goddess cave is a bad maneuver for anyone. We leave here; we're going straight to Johnny Chin's— where I hang my hat."

"Johnny Chin? Never heard of it or him or them," Pigtails tells us.

"Car wash chain," Bambi answers. "Be polite and let me finish, girl. Johnny Chin's is a big, long car wash you drive through. They have them in forty-eight states. I have an office in the back at the Summerlin location. Halfway through the wash tunnel there's a pause—a section without spinning brushes or spraying water. If you order the Mega Wash or the Supreme Wash, this is where the homeboys come out and spot-scrub your ride. In about thirty minutes, when Old School and I roll through, we hit that gap in the line; the homeboys come out and spot-scrub, and I will exit the car and go rest in my office. The wash continues, and Old School goes onward, and the gaggle waiting outside continues to chase Old School."

Pigtails stares at Bambi, stares at me, and then stares back at Bambi.

"I'll grab your grand, and we can swap outfits."

"But... don't you want to ask something?" Bambi asks.

"It's a good plan. Will you be able to sneak out of the car in the tunnel unnoticed? A girl can hope. You don't sound like you are afraid of being bait between here and Chin's. My conscience feels a lot better."

"I doubt that is what is causing you to be snippy," Bambi adds. "I wouldn't want to say goodbye to Old School either. Wherever you're going, I don't want to know, and I don't care. But he does. He wants you to get this win. I would be sad as hell to say goodbye to that. And you're right —whatever clowns are out there in the parking lot really will chase us down. If, by chance, they see me exit the vehicle and try to talk to me at all at Johnny Chin's, that's their demise and nothing on you, girl. Whether they see me or not, the chase after Old School continues and the attention is off you."

In a style similar to the old TV detective Columbo, Pigtails says, "I guess I do have a question. Once we change over, you two leave with the pack and get in the car and drive away. How far is Johnny Chin's? The followers are going to pounce. You know they are. Drive-by shooting, corner you into pulling over—any of that could go down. Don't make the drive to Johnny Chin's too long. Once they catch you two, the ruse is over, and they'll be hightailing back to this place if they figure out you were a decoy."

Pigtails is bullseye on point, as usual. I don't have an answer right away, but before I can say anything, Bambi answers, "You're right. You're dead-on correct. That's why, as soon as we leave, you need to go to the room I reserved, lock the door, and call a limo."

"Old School just said wait until I hear from him before I do that," Pigtails fires back, doing her stall-by-arguing routine again.

"Forget that he said that," Bambi answers. "One woman to another: as soon as we leave this room, you leave. Go straight to the room I rented. Call the limo while you're walking to my room."

Pigtails stays quiet at first, her mind running something.

Bambi stands and starts undressing right there. "Old School, hon, you are going to be costume director—outside party looking in and making sure we get the costumes right."

I turn my chair so my back is facing them. "Privacy while you undress. I'll turn back around when you say," I tell them.

"Okay, I guess this is it," Pigtails adds. "The

final step."

I can hear the impending goodbye in her voice—a tone that's sweet and heavy.

Twenty-nine

"**N**ow this is the final step," Bambi tells Pigtails and me.

All three of us stand at the door. I'm about to open it. Pigtails has just called for a limo. I feel like I want to throw up. The smell and taste of metal are stronger than before. Bambi's glances at me have been getting longer and fuller; I can see a sadness—she's certainly figured out I have a hidden wound of some kind. Any minute now, she'll say something.

"Don't hug me too hard, Old School," Pigtails tells me as she steps forward and hugs me. "You know I have issues."

I try not to choke up. I know she said that as an excuse to be gentle—she's worried about my wound.

Our hug ends.

The truth is, I don't want the hug to ever end.

I pull away from Pigtails and tell her, "I'll text you when we're on the road from here. And

I'll text again when we're rolling through the wash tunnel at Johnny Chin's."

Even Bambi looks a little choked up at our parting; the telltale sign is her wiping her cheeks. I like how her mascara runs—it reminds me of Alice Cooper.

Pigtails adds, "I'll text you as soon as I'm at the airport, and then again when I'm through the security gate."

I give Bambi a cursory nod. She shoulders the MOLLE pack, I open the door, and we exit the room.

The door shuts behind us. Bambi and I walk briskly down the hallway, side by side. In my head, I'm preparing for the trouble that's sure to come as soon as we step outside.

This is when Bambi—being a goddamn mind reader—waves at the security guard as soon as we reach the lobby.

The man walks over, and she says, "Look, handsome, my ex is a bit of a drama queen. My fear is that he's outside. Would you be a doll and walk us to our car?"

The security guard is all clogged up when he answers. I would be, too. Shit, Bambi's in combat boots, a mini-mini skirt, blue pigtails, oversized sunglasses, and a halter top that's barely holding things together.

My worry genes, on the other hand, are red-flagging a storm about Bambi being a little thicker and how her bigger boobs are noticeable compared with Pigtails. Bambi also doesn't have as many tatts as Pigtails.

We'll see.

Thirty

"How many?" I snap. I don't mean to snap. I need Bambi to confirm there are at least three carloads—the number of followers Pigtails and I had at the hotel. If any stayed back, that could be a problem when the limo arrives to pick up Pigtails, even though she's in full Red Riding Hood regalia.

My ideal scene is to have Eightball's whole army away from Pigtails—pursuing Bambi and me.

"I'm sure I see one on us, maybe two," Bambi tells me.

"I need there to be three or more. We had three cars full of followers back at the hotel—two generic sedans, like rentals, and a—"

"Easy, easy," Bambi cuts me off. "I'm sure they're all coming. Just drive us to Chin's. Drive mellow, too. Your girl will make it out and get to the airport just fine. The limo was on the way as soon as we left the room. The people you're worried about have no idea she'll be the blonde in the Riding Hood outfit. You have to admit, I look like your girl. When we walked out, I looked like your girl."

"I got worry genes," I answer.

"No shit, Sherlock. You really do, friend. Turn left up here, then right on Pebbles."

I can see Johnny Chin's coming up. We drive into the parking lot slowly, getting in line for the wash tunnel.

The wash tunnel is a long, warehouse-type building. The entire outside is painted red, white, and blue, set back from the street. There's a large parking area at the far end where attendants buzz from car to car like bees on blossoms. Halfway between the entrance and exit sits a kiosk with umbrellas, coffee, soda, hot dogs—everything to keep you distracted.

Once we're in line, rolling forward at a snail's pace, I use the mirrors to check each car behind us. I need to see our followers.

If they're not here, they're still back at the hotel.

"Look at the car two cars back," Bambi says. "Sedan with three or four knuckleheads in it. See that? Your plan worked."

I squint through the rear window, scanning the line of cars as best I can.

"I just see that one car," I finally tell Bambi. "Looks like a soccer mom and teens, not four knuckleheads ready to beat my ass and snatch the MOLLE pack they think is full of their money."

"Are the worry genes talking again? No need to answer. Remember *The Walking Dead*?"

"Absolutely. Zombie dystopia show. What does that have to do with right now?"

"You look and smell like a walker, Old School. You've been bleeding out this whole time, and that black hoodie and sweats hide it. Tell me I'm wrong."

I turn back toward the front. I'm not going to argue about my spiraling physical condition. I'm dead meat, and I know it.

I text Pigtails. I can feel Bambi watching me.

OLD SCHOOL
Hey, bro. We're
here at Chin's. Let
me know the good
news.

"I'm sure there's more," Bambi adds. "Since when do four dudes drive through a car wash together?"

I still don't see what she sees. That car two cars back looks like a mom with teens packed in for the tunnel.

"I just texted Pigtails. We'll see where she's at."

Bambi smirks. "I saw that. Pretty young girl like that lets you call her 'bro.' You two really bonded. Like father and daughter. Two soldiers in the trenches."

I don't answer. It hurts.

In the mirrors, I can only see four cars back, but the line has grown fast. Of the closest four, one looks like another follower. The driver and passenger look like linebackers—both faces tranced out on my Frank Montu car.

My body won't stop sweating. I reek of metal. Add chills on top of it. Sweating like a stuck pig, shivering like I'm in a freezer.

Pigtails finally messages back. No words. Just an emoji.

A smiling face with two hearts for eyes.

What does that mean?

The line creeps forward. We're almost in the wash tunnel.

"Too late to turn around now, Captain," Bambi says, reading my mind.

"What's the emoji with hearts for eyes mean?" I ask. "Never understood them. Bass-ackwards pictograms from three thousand years ago."

I show Bambi my phone.

She scrunches her face. "That's whack, buddy. She doesn't seem like the emoji type. What it is—she sees you as a dad. Since she probably never had one, she's saying thank you the only way she knows how."

I text Pigtails again.

OLD SCHOOL
Where're you at?

The line moves again. We're practically *in* the tunnel.

I can't stop replaying in my mind our past text messages. Bare minimum. No plans spelled out. This emoji isn't her style. My gut screams someone's using her phone.

Someone grabbed her.

That's what happened.

Pigtails finally responds.

> **PIGTAILS**
> **Hey. Sorry for being slow. I was paying the limo. Bet your ass the plan worked. Half the parking lot emptied out when you guys left. You had at least four cars follow you when you and the stripper left. I'm at the airport, in line for security. Quit worrying— you got an army on your ass now.**

I show Bambi the message with raised eyebrows.

"See?" she says. "Your girl's fine."

"It sounds like her... but also doesn't."

Bambi grins. "Go ahead—ask her something only she'd know. Burst your paranoia bubble. You've got Woody Allen–level neuroses, Old School."

I nod and type:

> **OLD SCHOOL**
> **I know I'm being**
> **paranoid, but**
> **just so I know**
> **it's you—humor**
> **me. Twenty-one**
> **years ago, I took**
> **my girlfriend and**
> **her daughter to**
> **Disneyland. What**
> **was the daughter's**
> **name?**

"Hey, boss," Bambi says. "We're in the tunnel next. Foot off the brake, neutral once the wheels are on the track. The porter'll ask what wash you want. Tell him the 'Mega Wash.' That's the one with spot scrubbers. That's where I slip out."

"Got it," I tell her.

No answer yet from Pigtails.

The correct answer is Becky. Come on, girl. You know that.

The attendant appears. I tell him we want the Mega Wash. He slaps a tag on the inside of my windshield.

Still no answer.

The track grabs the car. Sudsy water slams down. Bambi glances at my phone. "You look like a Disneyland dad," she says.

I don't respond. My heart's hammering. If it's not Pigtails texting, then what?

"What was the name of the girl you took to Disneyland—Pigtails?" Bambi teases.

"Becky!" I snap.

Brushes slam against the car.

"Becky? Son of a gun. Should've guessed. Goddamn, Pigtails looks like a Becky."

My phone dings.

PIGTAILS
A lucky girl named
Becky. Quit being
paranoid.

The brushes peel away. Mist parts. Three tattooed guys appear.

"This is where I get out," Bambi says. She hugs me, whispering, "That girl never had a good man in her life. She suspects, or is pretending, or whatever—you're her daddy."

"That's not Becky," I say stiffly.

"What's it hurt to let her believe she had one good man? Four days of being a dad when she needed one—that's something. Maybe it'll help her believe in men again. You're not losing anything."

I don't answer. My eyes burn.

Bambi slips out into the mist. "Don't be a puss, Old School. And get to a doctor," she mouths before the door shuts.

The car lurches forward, deeper into the wash.

Ten feet left before daylight. Ten feet to text Pigtails.

Then I'll have to bolt.

And I'll need to drag it as far away as a quarter tank will take me.

Thirty-one

**OLD SCHOOL
Thank you for
being you—my
daughter who
came along right
when I needed one
the most. I love
you, and I'm so
proud of you.**

N ow I am out of the wash tunnel.

I briskly wave the attendants away and put the car in drive. I floor it—as much as a person can floor an old Toyota Corolla—until I hit Dean Martin Drive. I get on Highway 15 going south. Plenty of spots along the highway to pull off the main track and head out into the desert, which is exactly what I will do once I get past empty and am running on fumes.

I have two gas tanks, and they're both close to running on fumes now. One gas tank belongs to the car, and the other is my cardiovascular system, bleeding out.

Once I settle into the fast lane, I start watching the rearview mirror, seeing who is keeping up, who looks familiar. In the back of my mind, I am waiting for Pigtails to answer back. I suppose a part of me knows that she will, and when she does, her words will break my heart open for the fiftieth time.

Dang it.

I have to toss this phone. When they catch me and kill me, they'll use anything they can from my burner phone to track down Pigtails.

I will take no chances.

My body's about to fold its cards. My side is on fire, and it feels heavy. My pants, on the wounded side, have been soaking wet since we first entered Johnny Chin's wash tunnel. The walk to the car with Bambi back at the hotel must've blown me open. There is the overwhelming taste of metal with every breath and every swallow. When I texted Pigtails a few minutes ago, tears came, and the tears weren't salty.

The tears were pennies.

In a Frank Montu heart-and-mind scene, I would text Pigtails in about eighteen hours—catch her cranky ass in Glasgow. Tell her how I breezed through urgent care and I'm on my way back to Santa Cruz.

Not now.

This phone's got to go. I'm not taking any

chance on anybody getting a bead on Pigtails.

I could memorize her burner number and text her from a different burner. I don't have cash right now, but there's always a way.

Who am I fooling?

This car is almost out of gas, and then I'll make them chase me into the desert inside this old body with blown gaskets, a major oil leak, and chunks of copper rattling around.

Using my knees to steer, I grab the burner. I take out the SIM card, swallow it, and then fling the phone out the window. I don't honestly believe anybody from Eightball's army, angrily scattered behind me, saw me fling the phone, but knowing the clearing at the end of the road is close has me feeling all new levels of neurotic.

I won't get the chance to read Pigtails' response to my last message.

What irony.

The one thing that bugged the crap out of me regarding that young upstart—she always got the last word... until now.

I pass the town of Jean and then Primm. Next is the Spring Mountain Pass.

By the time I reach the top of the pass, the needle on the fuel gauge is below E. Even after crossing the summit and cruising downward on built-up volition, the needle doesn't move.

This is it. Time to pull over, go into the desert, and make a run on foot.

I don't want to be put down in front of

others, sent into that good night right here on the side of Highway 15—all the families and L.A. people. And I want the chase to last as long as possible.

I deserve some dignity with this exit because I don't want it this time, and I am spending everything I can muster to hang in there for as long as possible—this headstart for Pigtails.

In the rearview mirror, I have been watching for followers. I know for sure there are three to five vehicles behind me that will follow me into the scrub and sand.

The car starts to slow. I give it some gas, a couple of lurches, more momentum, and then the gas is finally out.

There is a narrow and gravelly road coming up, the signs tell me.

JOPPY ROAD. HISTORICAL.
ANCIENT MAN SITE, 17 MI.

I slide the gear into neutral and steer the car onto the shoulder, then onto Joppy Road. I don't use the brake so the momentum can at least carry me off the shoulder of the highway and down the road a hundred meters or so.

I'm no Minotaur now. I am more like the trickle of a mountain stream that rolled and flowed and seeped until it faded out in the desert.

A red Explorer is the first to follow me off the highway, followed by a Ford Bronco–looking thing and a third ride I can't quite see because of the dust.

Reaching sideways, undoing the seatbelt, unlocking the door—just the pain from reaching knocks the wind out of me.

I finally get the car door open. I move like molasses climbing out.

I don't look in the direction of my followers.

I look to the right.

There's a gully.

I start limping toward the gully while at the same time shouldering the MOLLE pack.

Get down in the gully and run is my plan. Maybe all this dust and confusion will buy me some time.

I can hear a car door or two open and shut. Footsteps.

A fourth vehicle pulls in as I am running toward the gully. To get off the freeway completely and not block the others, they have to pull in deep. They almost hit me as I stumble these last few feet to the gully's berm and go over the side.

I hit the bottom of the gully face-first. My side explodes with more pain. I try to stay still and wait for the loss of consciousness.

No loss of consciousness.

I get up on my knees, ready to pick a direction to crawl.

"Go to the left," Jeanie's voice tells me. "Go to the left."

I turn to the left. I am not a good crawler.

I can't breathe, but I can hear and feel myself apologizing to Pigtails.

"Go into the tunnel; it goes under the highway," Jeanie's voice tells me.

I move forward to the mouth of a small flash flood drainpipe, placed so flash floods don't wash out Highway 15.

With the MOLLE pack on my back, I am too big crawling on my knees, so I move to a low crawl, just like my old Army boot camp days.

I pause about halfway into the mouth of the tunnel. The tunnel is dark, runs deep, and stinks of everything. I can only imagine snakes and rats, garbage, and the filthiest urban detritus washed and blown off the scaly skin of Las Vegas revelers rushing to and fro, chasing their vices.

"Get in there," Jeanie chides me. "You've got nothing to lose. Make them come get you. Go in and in. They want you, and they want what they think is in the pack. Go in. Be Grendel, be the Minotaur, whatever—just make them go deep to get to you."

I crawl and crawl. The pipe starts to narrow enough that I can feel the pack rubbing on the corrugated ceiling of the drain tunnel.

Rattlesnakes? Are they hiding in here to catch a break from the desert sun and ambush a rodent? If they are, I crawl right over them.

The narrowness of the pipe is so tight I can't move anymore. I can't breathe. And my side, with the hole and the copper in it, feels as solid as tissue paper in water.

"Read this," Jeanie tells me.

Her hand appears in front of me out of the dark, holding a cellphone so the screen is facing me, about six inches from my face.

"It's an update from our girl."

> **PIGTAILS**
> I don't know the
> deal you had with
> Ereshkigal. I told
> you that chick
> is weird, and I
> don't even know
> her. I know you
> were trying to
> forgive yourself
> and then maybe
> love yourself. You
> were such an ace
> at both missions,
> you actually had
> a lot of love to
> give me. You did
> everything a good
> dad would do, and
> you did it with
> love. I am sitting
> at the gate, safe.
> Yes, there is
> a kiosk here for
> both FedEx and
> UPS. I shipped
> pre-paids to a

hotel in Glasgow using both freight providers.

I want to imagine you are at the local urgent care or something similar. My bet is that you took all the baddies on a wild chase into the desert.

We'll be loading the plane soon. From now on, I will use a line from your playbook. When someone asks about my dad, I will tell them, "Love was good to me," and that I only knew my dad for four days, but he was the best man I ever met. Thank you for being you.

Thirty-two

"How long has it been?" she asks with a cute snort of a laugh. Her eyes are blue fire, and she's sucking down her cigarette like she's starving—the darling can't wait to light the next. "I see you right now, Frank Montu."

I can't remember what I'm supposed to be talking to her about or why I'm here. This is Ereshkigal—I know that much.

How did I get here? Am I still in the tunnel, hallucinating this? Where's Jeanie? She was talking to me.

"It's been four days, hot sauce," I tell her. I'm being snappy because she's asking questions we both know the answers to. She had me borrow a body so I could help Pigtails. I barely lasted ninety-six hours and flailed the whole way through.

"Good. You know how to count. In the eyes of eternity, you were barely gone a moment. You got over yourself in ways. I can see it."

We are at a truck stop in Barstow, where Route 66 and three other veins of forgotten

America converge. Outside the window, a big, fat WELCOME TO BARSTOW sign rolls by.

Some fucking purgatory thing.

I'm trying real hard not to stare at her cleavage, same as before. This isn't easy. Her skin is so white it is almost blue. Her blouse is buttoned low—way down in Mississippi-bayou-kind-of-low—and the fabric parts as it rises.

Her hair is the color of wet raven feathers, flowing around the borders of her face and down her shoulders into an alluvial fade across her upper chest. Ereshkigal could pass for marble. Her face still resembles Isabelle Boyer-Singer—the model for the Statue of Liberty artists—especially the nose, chin, and brow.

"You going to tell me the good news?" I ask.

A waitress appears out of my right periphery. She sets a lowball glass in front of me. I can smell the Maker's Mark. The glass holds a large square of ice and three fingers of deep amber heaven. The waitress steps back to her cart and brings me a ribeye.

The ribeye is still sizzling; a clump of butter slowly fans out and melts.

I don't wait for Ereshkigal to answer. "This is nice," I tell her. "No maggots. I suspect you need another favor. Bribery will get you anywhere with me. The good news I want is… I need to know the Glasgow scene."

"She made it. None of what you would call 'followers' are any wiser. You tied everybody up just fine."

"What's the favor, babe? I want to hear it."

"Look at you. I met you; you were Mr. Doom and Gloom—the Minotaur in the Labyrinth. A formidable beast who thinks he doesn't need to grow anymore, so he punches his own ticket. Now you've got some fire back in you."

Ereshkigal pauses, makes a clicking noise with her tongue, and raises her left arm. A young man runs out of the darkness—sixteen years old, if a day.

"Gorman, bring Mr. Montu a small mirror, please," Ereshkigal says.

The waif disappears and returns in less than a minute with a small Victorian mirror—gold trim, hand-painted decorative molding along the handle.

"Look at yourself, Mr. Montu," Ereshkigal tells me. "Can you see the suns and moons and the endless starry skies?"

I take the mirror. It's me—Francis Daniel Montu. I extend my arm and take in the whole body. Christ, I'm glowing. I've got my strapping thirty-year-old body.

"It's not like this, is it?" I ask.

"What do you mean, Montu? What you see is what you get."

"I mean, 3D reality, back in Santa Cruz. What do I look like there?"

"This is the Between Place, Frank. Here with me, this is you. The you of Santa Cruz is in the morgue and will be cremated. You go to Santa Cruz; everything you remember is there, but nobody will see you. Here in the Between Place, what seems to be, is—to those to whom it seems to be."

I reach down and grab the lowball. I sip it. It's cold, sweet, spicy, and it burns going down. I set the glass down and cut off a corner of the ribeye —the most fatty and succulent piece of meat I have ever seen. My Between-Place body is starving.

Good Lord, the steak is hot, salty, and slick with grease.

I lift another bump from the Maker's glass. "Okay, kitten, you going to ask your favor? Pitch it to me. I'm ready," I say.

"Maxine Patricia Kelly owns a business just shy of Goldfield, Nevada. A small resort, nine holes of golf, some hot springs, and a brothel with a dozen to twenty girls, depending on the season. Maxine is fifty-seven, and she built the business with her father. Now her father has left the physical realm for good. A couple of characters have been coming around—wanting freebies and food—and they're determined to take the business away from Maxine."

"That sounds about right. I'm not surprised," I say. "I suspect you want me to help, and you'll let me use the body of a washed-up addict or some such."

"Nathan Speed is eighty-seven, and he went to high school with Maxine's father. He's old, but mobile. He spent years in the Merchant Marines, and ever since he retired, he's been drinking himself to death."

"Another halfway-house whack-job," I add. "What's in this for me?"

"Don't be a prude. Without help, I'll have to pick up Maxine myself next week. I'm enjoying watching her have some success with what she and her father created. I want to see her win."

"When, and what's in it for me?" I press.

"Dear Nathan's been trying to put a cork in the bottle since yesterday—this his fiftieth visit to rock bottom. His body is convulsing and having seizures because of withdrawals. He will have a large seizure in exactly thirty-three minutes. This gap in consciousness will be your entrance into his body."

After a long pause, I ask, "I see. Out of the pan and into the skillet. You skipped the what's-in-it-for-me part earlier."

"The same reward that's in it for all of us: you get to seek and find that Inexhaustible Love that created you, while seeking from a limited and perhaps alien point of view."

"What if I want a vacation?"

"A vacation from what—learning about yourself?"

"This whole guardian angel racket, whatever I was doing. I'm not good at that."

"You are so full of it. I'm no guardian angel —never was. Since you work for me, you aren't either."

I don't say anything. I sip my bourbon. I wait. There's more. She wants to give me a mom lecture. I can feel it.

"You don't have to confess this. I already know. You had a real hoot helping Pigtails. If I sent you back to that morning four days ago, right before the Luger scene, your body would feel like an overly tight shoe—too small. Expansion happened. All the trouble Pigtails gave you, you enjoyed it."

About The Author

Adam Patrick Donovan

On the edge of the Pacific, Adam lives a life of quiet California magic with his wife and an overfed tortoise. His mission is to blur the line between the detective's shadow and the sorcerer's secret, crafting novels meant to be swallowed whole in a single day.

Books By This Author

Corpus Cacao

When Maggie picks up a strange hitchhiker on a lonely stretch of road, she has no idea what she's letting into her life—or what he's leaving behind.

The chocolates are exquisite. Intoxicating.
And they summon something that knows Maggie better than she knows herself.

Servius is beautiful, attentive, and devoted to her pleasure in ways no human lover has ever been. With each bite, Maggie slips further into a private paradise where desire is effortless and consequences feel far away. But pleasure always has a cost—and the chocolates demand more than Maggie ever expected to give.

As her addiction deepens, Maggie crosses lines she can never uncross, convinced she can control the ritual, the craving, and the thing that comes when she calls.

She's wrong.

Corpus Cacao is a dark erotic horror novella about desire as devotion, pleasure as ritual, and the terrible price of mistaking appetite for love.
Seductive, grotesque, and utterly unforgiving, this story lingers long after the last bite.

Easy Breezy

Buzz Birdy is your average Joe—perfectly unremarkable, the ideal cover for a thriving private investigation business. Next door is Tippy Newmark, the sun-kissed California surf Barbie, always drawn to the worst kinds of heartthrobs. Buzz has long harbored feelings for her, but he's content with their friendship... until Tippy vanishes.

Her disappearance goes unnoticed by everyone except Buzz. Driven by a gut feeling that something is terribly wrong, he faces an adversary that's always four steps ahead, stronger, and relentless in its pursuit to keep Tippy hidden.

Caught in a deadly game of cat and mouse, can Buzz's love and ingenuity break through the web of danger and deceit to rescue Tippy? Or will the shadows prove too formidable?

Same Set Of Fleas

$3.5 million in gold. One night to steal it. A thousand eyes watching.

Marvin is a pro at getting in and out—and so is his adrenaline-junkie girlfriend, Elektra. But Tom's sister's house isn't a normal score. It's a maze of "disturbo" art, psychological traps, and a basement that shouldn't exist.

When the rules are broken, the statues start to bite.

Set in the shadows of the Santa Cruz Mountains, Same Set of Fleas is a dark, supernatural crime thriller where noir greed collides with skin-crawling horror. If you like high-stakes heists that curdle into something much worse, this one will stay with you.

Squeeze

Terry Saff and his cousin Trigger don't get along well. Terry would also love to get a break from his wife, Gretchen. That's when the three reluctant partners decide to rob Bucky's Auto-Rama—a car dealership notorious for "cash only" deals and having plenty of cash on hand. Terry dreams of losing both his wife and cousin while making off with the swag. There are just two speedbumps in the way: no loyalty amongst thieves, and Bucky's otherworldly concubine has a penchant for violence.

Putting Janice By

James is at his breaking point. His wife, Janice, is dying, and after trying every possible cure, they are out of options. Desperate, a close friend urges James to seek help from an unconventional source: a conjure woman named Strega. To his surprise, her magic works--until James makes the mistake of shortchanging Strega's payment. Now, something far more dangerous than illness has come to collect what he owes, and it won't stop until it gets what it's after.

Molly Malone

Molly Malone. Former Marine, former sheriff's deputy, tough as nails woman's woman. She has her PI shingle hung in San Francisco's Tenderloin District, and she could not be prouder—she rolls with the beasts and soars with the angels. Molly takes a case that seems too easy, until it's not, and lovers behave badly...and the dead become undead.

Borrowed Angel

June killed her boyfriend—gorgeous, washed-up, underwear model Todd—after catching him being a rake...again. In a desperate attempt to undo her actions, she seeks out a reclusive local known for having a peculiar tunnel on his property. This tunnel, for a price, promises a one-way trip back to the previous Thursday.

On the other side of the tunnel, June finds Todd is very much alive, and so is a nasty doppelganger named June Second. Additionally, June's not the only one delighted with the tunnel's secret. This other tunnel user, Julius, is keen on erasing June's existence as opposed to sharing.

Amidst this chaos, June's sole ally is an Old-World jeweler—handsome, wealthy, and unhappily married. The jeweler's consistency and robust love for June provide the only solace and stability she has as she races to survive and find her way home. Can June keep the jeweler alive, and can she take him with her when she leaves?

Globes

Jack is a boilerplate tough guy, an unlicensed PI, and a part-time skip tracer with a predilection for strip clubs. It's in this neon-lit world where Jack meets Rhiannon, a pole dancer with a sharp mind and the perfect recipe for robbing banks: the "Eight Laws of Successful Bank Robbing."

Their partnership ignites into an intoxicating fire, white-hot. All is love between thieves, until Jack colors outside the lines of Rhiannon's "Eight Laws" and draws the attention of a thing of nightmares with an inexhaustible appetite for torment.

Dinner For Nic

AJ, Mittens, and Sparky are far from the best grifters, badger game players, sneak thieves, and safecrackers, but they give it their all. When they spot the perfect safecracking opportunity at a greasy spoon café on Main Street America, it seems too good to pass up. What they don't account for, however, is the café's real owner: a being of unspeakable menace.